THE SOUL GATHERERS

Thirteen Western Tales

THE SOUL GATHERERS

Thirteen Western Tales

CHARLIE STEEL
Tale-Weaver Extraordinaire

CONDOR PUBLISHING, INC.
Lincoln, Michigan

THE SOUL GATHERERS
Thirteen Western Tales

by Charlie Steel

May 2020

Library of Congress Control Number: 2020937947

ISBN-13: 978-1-931079-34-1

Condor Publishing, Inc.
PO Box 39
123 S. Barlow Road
Lincoln, MI 48742
www.condorpublishinginc.com

Printed in the United States of America

DEDICATION

This book is dedicated to my mother, Frances, and my father, Glenn.

Both were strict and demanded at a very early age that their children work hard and do their very best in all things. Their way of life instilled discipline and kindness to others. They believed in Heaven and Hell and living a faithful life. If one walked the straight and narrow, there was no room for wrongdoing.

TABLE OF CONTENTS

THE DEVIL, THE GAMBLER, AND THE GIRL

Jack Diamond had gambled in nearly every smoke-filled, liquor-soaked saloon in the West. Jack was born an intelligent and handsome boy, and with his quick mind, he could have become anything he wanted—a teacher, a college professor, a doctor, an engineer, or any other desirable profession. As a child, his instructors, as well as his parents, had high hopes for the bright-eyed lad. But a darker side took over the youth's God-given talents, and by the time he was eighteen, he had spent many a lantern-lit night holding cards around crowded tables.

From Montana to Texas, from Oklahoma to California, he had made his living being slicker with cards than the average man. His fingers could feel and memorize the hidden faces with a sensitive consciousness all their own. And his quick mind could remember each card played, every combination, and thus the odds were increased to his side. But still, gambling was an iffy business at best, and when playing honestly, Lady Luck was a fickle companion.

From time to time, when the cards weren't with him, he had used his skill to shuffle a winning hand. And sometimes, not often, he was called out for it. During those tense moments, he would try his best to subdue the situation. Most times successfully, but not always. On more than one occasion, it had ended with a derringer in hand, and a dead adversary lying across green felt, scattered cards, and blood-splattered greenbacks.

The endless procession of towns and saloons, late nights spent in smoke-filled rooms with the stale smell of spittoons, tobacco, and alcohol, made the color of Jack's face an unhealthy pallor. His once clear eyes and smooth, taut skin were beginning to wrinkle. Hands, once steady and firm, began to tremor. Memories of countless games, and innumerable gunfights, and the faces of death, were eating at the clouded consciousness of the man. In bed, when sleep came, there were nightmares.

Gambling became less successful. The elegant outfits he always wore faded with repeated use and became drab and threadbare. Jack was losing his touch and his nerve, deadly for any gambler. He was becoming weary of his profession and of life itself. He was without a friend in the entire world, a lost soul all alone in a sea of humanity. Jack was well aware that his entire life had become nothing but a meaningless existence. Abhorring alcohol during his career, he now was turning to it for solace. It became the medication that allowed him fitful moments of sleep.

One late night, after breaking even at the card table, he made his way up to the single room in a rundown hotel somewhere in a town in New Mexico. The name was unknown to him, and if told, he would neither care nor be concerned. This particular night Jack was in a fit of remorse. The dead faces of the many innocents he had killed over a manipulated card game wavered in his consciousness—faces he could not forget, and that would not go away. Without awareness, he blurted out drunkenly his desperate thoughts.

"I'd sell my soul to the Devil for one night's good sleep and to never remember another dead man's face."

The Indians who once inhabited the vast western deserts of New Mexico and the great mountains believed in the power of all things. Here was an ancient and mysterious land, never to be fully conquered by man. Mysteries still abounded, the magic of the country would always pervade human spirits. It was a vast and arid place full of wonder.

When Jack Diamond finished speaking, a deadly silence occurred, followed by a terrific wind that came with a low moaning sigh. It increased to a howling rush that shook the hotel and the very room where Jack set his weary body down. For one second, upon the lumpy mattress, a flicker of recognition of the mysterious sound came to the mind of the man and then was lost as Jack closed his eyes and slept.

There were no spectral images of gaping mouths and twisted figures, gasping out their last breaths. On this night, he saw no man in his death throes across a table of scattered cards. No faces haunted him of angry men who accused him of sleight of hand with colored pasteboards. The images of ghost-white faces remembered in the late hours did not haunt him as they had for so many years. Nor did his mind and body wake him in the black of night for a sip of the fiery brew. For in the past, only liquor, a product more of the Devil's making, could soothe his jangled nerves.

This was the first night in years where haunting dreams did not repeat themselves during the dark hours. Still, his consciousness remembered and regretted that he had turned away from the teachings of his parents. So long ago he had shown scholarly promise of becoming a man of great success. Instead, he had taken the easy path, using his sharp mind to count cards, to cheat his fellow man, to turn to avarice in pursuit of a wastrel's life.

When Jack awoke, he felt refreshed. It was the first time in years he had slept the night through. There was something unusual about the atmosphere of the room, and there was a distinct sulfur odor. The gambler rose up, and sitting at a chair was a darkly dressed man. Swarthy of appearance, the stranger was painfully slim. Dark skin stretched tightly over his skull. His black hair came down on his broad forehead, and above each temple, a tuft of hair stood up in a pointed fashion. Black eyes with a dancing yellow flash looked back intensely. Boney, long skeletal fingers held a deck of cards. The hands moved, the cards whirred in a deft and fancy shuffle.

"How about a game?" asked the dark stranger.

"Who are you?"

"A gambler, like yourself. I believe you made a wish. I came to fulfill it. Now, how about the card game? I don't have much time. We'll play one hand, and winner takes all."

"I'm afraid I am short of funds," said Jack.

"No matter. One game, your soul against—how did

you put it? Oh yes—'for one night's good sleep and to never remember another dead man's face.'"

"Is this some kind of joke?" asked Jack, now rising from his bed, still fully dressed.

"I assure you, it is not."

A dark curtain covered a window, and Jack walked to it and drew it back to look out. Intense light beamed inwardly, and the cadaverous man waved his hand. Jack turned and saw it. There was a loud snap of the boney fingers, and the curtain by itself slammed together, shutting out the light.

"If you don't mind," clipped the stern voice of the stranger. "We'll dispense with that."

Jack observed the intruder and knew without a doubt that he was being visited by a creature of supernatural abilities.

"I would not win against a man of your talents," said Jack in surprising calmness.

"Come, Jack, at least try to play a good game. You and I both know very well that with the life you have led, I will have your soul anyway. What's the difference if it is now or later?"

"If that is so, why play for it at this very moment?"

"I have my quota," answered the dark stranger in his smooth and soothing voice. "And…well…there is always the chance that you could change…a slim chance, of course, but free-will has always been a delicate matter in dealing with human lives."

"Why have you come? I mean…at this exact time?"

"You invited me, Jack. We…I…never come unless invited. Let us play. Your wish has been granted. For as long as you live, you shall never have another nightmare, and you will sleep like an infant without a conscience."

"How long will that be?"

"Jack!" repeated the strange visitor in his slippery voice. "Jack! Is this the same man who fretted and wished for peace and death? Come now. There is no time to dally."

"And if I refuse to play?"

"Look at yourself in the mirror, Jack."

The gambler turned to a framed glass, and as suggested, looked at his image. Behind him reflected in the mirror was the chair, table, and wall, but not the dark stranger.

"Ten years have melted off you in one night's sleep," purred the Prince of Darkness. "Your eyes are clearer, and you even have a bit of color in your cheeks. Just think what a month of such rest could do for you."

"Do I have a choice?" asked Jack, walking to the door and now having regret for invoking the Devil's name.

"No!" he shouted. "Step outside that door, and I will visit upon you a thousand curses. Your death will be an agonizing one, I assure you!"

Reluctantly, Jack Diamond returned and sat on the edge of the bed. The dark man slid over a small table and chair, sat down, and began to shuffle. Cards whirred.

"Five-card draw is the game," said the stranger in a devilish voice.

When the five cards lay before him, Jack raised them. He had two eights and two aces. Jack laid aside a deuce. Then came a scream of a female from the next room, followed by the crashing of furniture. Jack arose, derringer in hand.

"That is not your affair!" shouted the Prince of Darkness,

standing up and blocking the door to the hotel room.

"I haven't yet lost all my decency!" said Jack, and he pushed the slim visitor aside.

The gambler felt sudden heat on his hands, and smoke actually billowed from the dark suit of the boney man. Again came the sulfur smell. Jack grabbed for the knob and thrust open the door. He ran into the hallway and to the adjacent hotel room.

"I warn you!" shouted the slim dark figure. "There will be consequences!"

Jack took hold of the door handle of the room from which the noise was obviously emanating. It would not turn, the mechanism was locked. With his shoulder, he slammed against the door, and it did not budge. The girl screamed again, and Jack thrust twice more, each time with increasing force. The jam, which held the metal lock and latch, broke, and the door swung inward. Two men were subduing a lady. One was tying her hands behind her, while the other was attempting to gag her mouth.

"That's enough!" shouted Jack. "What's going on here?"

"Muff, umph, umph," mumbled the gagged woman.

"Untie her and remove that rag!" ordered Jack, holding the derringer on the ruffians.

The two strong men eyed their adversary warily.

"This is none of your business!" shouted one of them angrily.

"I'm making it mine! Now untie her!"

One of the abductors reached inside his coat, and a gun and shoulder holster were exposed. Jack shot, and the bullet struck the man in the arm. He stopped reaching for the pistol and, instead, held his hand to a dripping wound.

The other man pulled the gag from the lady's mouth.

"They hired me," said the woman. "They promised room and board if I would clerk. But after I moved in, they told me I had to do more. I'll never turn to that!"

"This hussy owes the boss money," said the bully without the wound.

"I do not!" she protested.

Jack looked at the thugs. He could see from a lifetime of experience that these were toughs hired by the hotel owner to perform nefarious deeds. The woman in question was attractive, but like him, she had seen better times. She still held some of her good looks and figure despite her age. No doubt, she was in the same condition as him, desperate and low of funds.

"She owes money for food and the hotel room," said the wounded man. "The boss will pay heck, Mister, if we don't come with the dame or the money."

"How much?" asked Jack.

"You mean, you would help this…"

"How much?"

"Thirty dollars!" blurted out the man holding his shoulder.

"Untie her," said Jack, reaching in his rumpled coat, finding a leather wallet, and pulling nearly the last of his money from its folds. Jack selected three tens and held them out. The nearest tough grabbed for the cash.

"Mister!" shouted the wounded fellow. "Las Vegas, New Mexico, won't be healthy for the two of you. You better clear out, or…"

"Just get going," said Jack, still pointing the derringer at the men.

They left the room, and one of them slammed the door. It crashed against the broken jam, failed to latch, and swung open a few inches.

"Thank you," said the woman, staring with grateful hazel eyes. "They lied to you. I worked downstairs at the hotel desk. This room came with the job. But thank you. Who knows what…"

"It's alright," said Jack. "But you and I better clear out of here. I don't think it will be safe."

There came a distinct sulfur smell, and then the door silently swerved open. There, before the woman and Jack, stood the skeletal man in black.

"Have you forgotten something?" purred the man menacingly.

"No," said Jack. "I haven't forgotten. But for your information, Mister Mephistopheles, or whoever you are, I'm not playing. In fact, I've given up cards for life."

"Too late!" shouted the dark fellow.

"If it is," said Jack. "The first move is up to you."

"Who's that?" asked the woman. "He looks and smells awful!"

"Pay him no mind," said Jack. "As long as you live a clean life, you have nothing to fear from him!"

Jack put away his derringer and waited for the girl. He watched as she gathered a few items of clothing and placed them in a carpetbag. Jack went forward and shoved the man in black away from the entrance of the door. Upon contact, again, there was the sense of heat on his hands and the sulfurous smell. The former gambler went to his room and got his packed valise. He came back for the attractive female and watched her as she cautiously stepped around the emaciated fellow. The woman and Jack, bags in hand, began to walk down the hotel hallway and towards the stairs.

"This isn't the end of this!" shouted the gaunt figure in black.

"It is, as far as I'm concerned," said Jack. "She and I are going straight."

There was a cursing exclamation, the exact meaning escaping the ears of man and woman. And when they came to the top of the stairs, they heard a loud cracking sound. When Jack and the lady turned, all that was visible where the dark stranger had stood, was a gray wisp of smoke.

*1st Printing, *THE LAKESHORE GUARDIAN*, June 2019

DEATH AND THE DEVIL COME
FOR AN OLD MAN

Xavier P. Horace seemed to waste the last days of his life in pure and selfish idleness as he waited for death. Waking in his bed, he lay there a long while feeling the aches and pains of his aged body. As the sunlight crept higher through his bedroom window, and finally fell upon his cracked and lined face, the heat of it stirred the old man to rise.

It was a struggle to sit up and move his legs over the edge of the bed. A boy or a younger body would have done it without thinking. Still, every movement of an aged person took effort and pain, and with that, the acknowledgment of that pain. The old man groaned, grabbed for his pants from the wooden chair next to the bed, and put them on. Standing up, he fastened a belt around his thin waist.

Shuffling into the kitchen of the decrepit cabin, Xavier managed to pick up kindling and jam it into the firebox of the cookstove. Then he struck a lucifer and dropped it on the splinters. It didn't take long for flames to rise up. Putting the heavy firebox lid back down, he poured water in a tall pot, added fresh coffee, set it on the hot stove, and waited for the sound of boiling. When he thought the process was done, he poured himself a cup of the steaming brew, straining out the grounds with a rag placed over his mug. Tossing the cloth strainer aside, he took his coffee and went out onto the porch.

The old man sat down on the raggedy cushion of his favorite chair. As he looked out over the landscape, the open grasslands and tall mountains, he could barely make out the straight hash of Fisher's Peak. It had been years since he was able to visit the cliff that stood guard over the town of Trinidad. He would never see that wild town again. Then, as always, he went into a sort of trance and began to reminisce.

It sure was hard, he thought, *being saddled with a name like Xavier. Seems like I always ended with a bruised fist and a broken nose. Reckon, maybe I shouldn't have been so quick to fight. Don't seem right, ma and pa giving me that name. Sure didn't leave me feelin' charitable.*

As the old man sat there, pondering his life, he thought about the last words exchanged with his parents. They were harsh words, and he knew he wouldn't be back. The day after he turned fifteen, young Xavier P. Horace ran from home, went east, and joined the Union Army. He signed on as drummer boy to the first outfit that would take him.

He would never forget that date. It was June1861 when he enlisted with the 1st Regiment Kansas Volunteer Infantry.

I wasn't more than a fool kid, thought Xavier. *Those men and all them boys, 106 of them, dying there at Wilson's Creek. Sure no glory in that.*

The carnage and screams thundered and raced round and round in his brain.

T'was the same with Vicksburg. So many dead. I grew up then and went by Horace after that. Too bad I picked up that sniper's rifle.

Xavier lifted the coffee cup, took a drink, then sat sloshing the dark liquid in circles, mirroring the churning of his thoughts. Despite his age, every day it was the same; he recalled the war and killings that would not let him forget.

Uncanny how I remember them battles and dates. Vicksburg, May 22, 1863. I got shot in the right arm, and for the first time, I stepped away to collect myself. Bound up that wound, and wondered if I was gonna make it through that war. I come to the conclusion that humankind was not grown up enough to govern itself. I reckon I was right, war is just plumb stupid.

Xavier's eyes closed and he drifted off into sleep, his chin resting on his thin chest.

In his sleep, he remembered standing there, holding his right arm. That's when Colonel George Washington Deitzler himself came to talk.

"Son, are you that Horace fellow I heard about with the Sharps?"

"Yes, Sir!" I answered.

I tried to salute, but my armed pained somethin' fierce.

"Corporal, you go get that arm attended to and report back to my headquarters."

"Yes, Sir!" I replied.

I was such a thick-headed lad then, all smiles and

willing to please. I did as he told me and returned.

"Boy," said Colonel Deitzler. "I heard about you and that rifle of yours. I've got a special mission. Are you up to it, lad?"

As a drummer boy, I wished to be all growed up and become one of them sergeant's with them chevrons. I reckon a feller ought to be careful what he wishes. From that moment on, I killed far too many men.

The old man woke up with a start. The intense reverie of remembrances left Horace with a fierce headache. Drinking several swallows of the strong cold liquid, he put his cup down on a nearby stand and rubbed at his temples with thin arthritic fingers. Deeply tired of his thoughts, but totally unable to control them, Horace sat there numb with regret. The grim expression and tight jaws made his wrinkles all that more pronounced.

Sitting on the porch, he went into a coughing fit, his first for the day. After several long minutes, it stopped, and there was blood on his handkerchief. The coughing, along with the cancer in his lungs, was getting worse.

From the fields came running a mangy longhaired cur of a dog, its mottled-brown color made it blend in with the landscape. The hound was old but still managed a steady lope. When it came to the porch, it slowed, climbed up on the steps, and curled at the feet of the old man. The dog began licking its chops. Around the edges of its mouth was blood and bits of rabbit fur.

"I see you had a successful breakfast, hound," said Horace. "Doing better than me, old fellow. There was a time when I would have beat you to a hunt and food, but that's a long while ago."

Not so far in the past line of the cur was wolf's blood. In answer to the man, the hound raised back his head. Instead of a bark, came a long, slow, blood-curdling howl, similar to that of his ancestors. The old man adjusted his sore rump on the chair's cushion and attempted a smile, a rare thing indeed, for Horace. Then he dangled a free right hand and gently rubbed the head of the animal.

"You're the only friend I got, boy. Thanks for sticking around. It's more than I deserve—'specially since you have to find your own food these days."

Horace took several more drinks of his coffee and finished it. Desiring more, he was just too tired, too weak, and too lazy to get it. Besides, the hound was at his feet, and he did not want to disturb the honor of his presence. Then another coughing jag began, and it seemed to go on forever. This time, when it stopped, there was a copious amount of blood. It was on the handkerchief, his mouth, and dripping down onto his bare and bony chest.

The part-wolf, part-hound, looked up and then howled his grief.

"You see it too, don't you, boy?" said the old man. "Today might be the day."

Without moving, the cur and the old man sat out the better part of the morning. Both enjoyed the warmth of the ever-rising sun. At exactly noon, Horace finally got up and creaked his way back into the kitchen. He went to make another cup of coffee and fetch a bite of jerky. The only thing on the old man still in good shape were his teeth. Chewing on the salty meat, he swallowed a short piece.

When finished, the coughing started all over again.

When it stopped, there was more blood. Breathing became harder, and his chest ached and pained fiercely. Horace, feeling dizzy, forgot about the stove or another cup of coffee, and he ambled his way back to his cushioned chair on the porch. He went to sit down but instead collapsed into it, hitting his head against the wall of the cabin. The blow to the back of the head was hard enough to break skin. With difficulty, he raised his arm and hand and felt the wound. He brought it back covered in blood.

Another coughing fit began, and it went on and on. Near the end of it, Horace could barely breathe. It took every measure of him to endure the pain. Horace's vision blurred, and before him, he thought he saw a wavering dark object. It looked something like black smoke. Then came the smell of sulfur. There was a clapping sound, and the smoke instantly took the form of a human. The wolf-dog on the porch howled once. There was a snap of fingers from the figure, and the hound ran away.

"I've been expecting you," whispered Horace.

"It is seldom anyone ever expects me," said the dark figure. "Perhaps you are mistaken."

"No," replied Horace. "Along with my nightmares and daydreams, I've seen a wavering shadow. Given my past, I had no illusions what that meant."

"Come now, you must have had hope of redemption," said the figure. "Most folks do delude themselves so."

"I have held no such hope," replied Horace.

"Then, you know what I am here for."

"Yes, to take me to a place for punishment."

"Well said, Horace. But let me tell you, it was not I, nor any other force, that made you a soldier and killer of men. Nor, to choose to live up on this mountain. When have you ever helped your fellow being?"

"All my life there were few who welcomed my presence," exclaimed the old man. "Only real friend I ever had was that tortured wolf-hound that you just sent running."

"Come now," said the dark entity. "Everyone you met, you made an enemy."

"I tried as a youngster, I tried as a young soldier, and as a man. It did no good. Best decision I made was to come up here and leave people alone."

"Huh," replied the dark stranger. "Stop this self-pity and beg for your life."

The old man took a breath, and in it came the strong smell of sulfur. Horace found himself coughing and unable to breathe. Slowly, the aged fellow collapsed to the floor of the porch and gasped his final breath.

From across distant mountain tops blew a cool wind, and it swept through the prairie and towards Xavier P. Horace's cabin. Along with the wind came a white image that gently drifted over the stricken corpse.

"Oh no, you don't," snarled the dark shape of the Devil, now transforming itself into wavering smoke.

"You did not prove this man's guilt," said the pleasant voice of the Angel.

"I did, I did!" shouted the Devil.

"No, he told you, he chose to live alone and not hurt anyone."

"But he was a killer! More than a hundred lives, he took!"

"Granted," said the Angel, "He killed many, but that was in war. We admit he has done little good in this world, or for his fellow humans, but still, he made a decision on how to live his later life."

"It was how he killed that condemns him. I demand my right to take what is mine!" declared the Devil.

"I'm sorry," said the Angel, its aura briefly increasing in intensity and then fading. "This man has been judged, and he goes with us."

"How can you possibly come to such a conclusion?" argued the Devil. "There is not one man, woman, or child—not one living being—who will stand up for this killer!"

"Ahhh, but you are wrong. Even now, as we waver in the presence of this man's soul, his absolution has been made."

"But how?" asked the Devil.

From across the grass-filled yard of the old cabin came the mangy hound. Afraid, its tail between its legs, the wolf-dog crept slowly forward. Shivering at the two entities before it, it still moved ahead and up to the old man's body. It laid down and put its head on the man's chest and whined in grief at his master's passing.

SATAN VISITS THE WEST

One of the favorite places on earth for Satan to visit is the American West. It has all the characteristics that favor his disposition. There are the scorpions, the various poisonous snakes, the wolf, the bear, and the mountain lion. The warm-blooded creatures might be majestic, but they also have teeth and claws. In that way, their sometimes savage behavior is very favorable to the soul-taker who likes the color red. Then, there is the coyote who hunts in packs and whose combined ferocity matches few other creatures. And...of course...the main reason for visiting— the extreme heat. A lot of the American West is high desert where it seldom rains. Often the hot wind blows like a furnace from Hell and with it, the incessant dust.

It was on one such hot, dry day that the malevolent personage himself took shape as a black cloud slipping in with the wind blowing the beige dust across the arid land. After a time, the dark vaporous form came to settle on a rock, a giant granite stone formed by the fires of the earth millions of years before. And below that massive crag lay a little cabin. In fact, once it may have been a sturdy abode, but now, after years of exposure, it was more like a shack.

It leaned away from the constant southwesterly wind that decomposed the wood. Decay was one of Satan's favorite interests, and this little wooden affair looked like it was ready to fall over at any moment.

To the surprise of the dark being resting upon the hot rock, a man appeared from the shack. *What kind of human would be living way up here in this isolated and dry high desert?* Satan was curious. Here was a soul he had missed, one that had escaped the collective knowledge of those who worked under him. The Devil himself would investigate. This must indeed be a curious specimen of humanity.

On the other side of the shack, the old man worked at harnessing an ancient cart to a cantankerous pony. It was a four-wheeled affair, short, like the Mexican wagons below the border. In the back was a huge wooden barrel, almost as tall as the man himself and twice as wide.

"Con sarn it! You bag of bones! Don't you see if you don't let me harness this here conveyance, Rosy, you and me won't have no water. And with no water, you and me ain't a-gonna last very long in this here heat and dust. Now honey, COOPERATE!"

"Neyyyyyyy," replied Rosy.

The Devil watched in wavering form beside a corner of the wooden structure. The dust storm, increasing in intensity by the raging wind, hid the dark shape. The powerful deity from below became even more interested. By concentrating, Satan learned about this human creature. It was a natural attribute, and like osmosis, it came to the ruler of darkness, the entire life history of this poor unfortunate excuse for a human being.

The man's life story was a bit more unique than those other paltry souls that selfishly crawled over the earth. This man-creature was not like the others. He did not use his free will to destroy. Here was an independent human being who had nearly lived out his life in peace and quiet, neither committing right nor wrong. His footprint upon this earth hardly created an impression. This was the reason his soul had escaped the powerful personage who lorded over the Dominion of Darkness. But this human would escape no longer, for Satan himself was here to entice his soul. For his own particular amusement, perhaps there was yet a way to tip the scales of this old man in favor of eternal damnation.

It took effort, and it drained the power of Satan to remain in this neutral territory for too long, but for the first time in years, he lingered. He began to concentrate his energy and took form as a human with reddish skin, black hair swept up at peculiar angles, and wearing a dark suit. Out from the corner of the cabin stepped the man in black. His presence was accompanied by a sulfurous smell that blew into the nostrils of the old man and horse. Both man and animal turned in surprise and one grunted and the other snorted.

"I see I take you unaware," said Satan. "But I am lost, and I have come to ask for guidance."

"Where's your hoss and your gear, fella?" shouted the old man above the wind.

"A breeze startled my animal, and it fled with my possessions," lied the creature in black.

At that moment, the storm blew harder and hotter, and

dust swirled so heavily and fiercely that it became difficult to breathe.

"Inside!" shouted the old man.

Giving up on harnessing his beloved Rosy to the wagon, the old man took hold of her halter and led her into a lean-to on one side of the shack. The dark man followed. Here the wind and most of the dust were blocked. The old man and the pony took in breaths of cleaner air, and both sneezed.

"Stay here, Rosy," shouted the man above the wind. "We'll go for water and supplies later."

Shutting the door to the lean-to, the man ran for his cabin, holding a kerchief to his nose. The wind blew at the opening of the shack, and the Westerner struggled with the door as it nearly escaped his grasp. The stranger slipped in, and the old man followed, closing the entrance with great difficulty.

Dust hung in the dim light of the shack. One dirty, stained window let in light, and dust particles danced through its piercing rays. The old man felt the peculiar presence of his guest, and it was not pleasant. Turning, the old fellow gazed a short moment at this being. His faded blue eyes took in the cadaverous body, the tufted black hair untouched by the wind, and the peculiar stain of red upon the being's skin.

The old man shook with a kind of chill, despite the heat, and every one of his senses warned him that this was no ordinary man.

"Say," said the oldster, "not to criticize, but there's something off about you, feller."

"Why, whatever do you mean?" asked Satan, a sardonic smile creeping over his lips.

Not liking the sun's stilted rays coming through the dirty window, the creature snapped his fingers, and the dusty curtain closed, making the cabin darker. Still, through various holes and cracks, rays of light managed to penetrate along with the blowing dust.

"Ahh," said the man. "It's you. I wondered what you would look like."

"I tend to take on the form in which you imagine me to be."

"My time has come?" asked the old man.

"No, not yet, but it is close."

"I have tried to make a quiet life for me and Rosy on this mountain slope. I bother no one, and no one bothers me. Me and Rosy like it that way."

"You are rather fond of your animal friend?"

"She's my only companion, through thick and thin. Mind you, she's my second. Myself, unfortunately, living longer than my first."

"And what do you do with your days?"

"Why me and Rosy enjoy them. There's something fine about clear blue skies, constant sunlight, and heat. We admire quiet, the views, and the fresh air. You just might say we like our lives the way it is."

"I see. And…"

"Say, what is this? Some kind of inquisition I heard about?"

"You are an interesting subject, Mr. Walter Miller."

"So you know my name?"

"And everything else about you."

"How come?"

"May I say," said the dark figure, "that it is a gift that comes with our trade."

"The taking of souls?"

"Yes, very astute."

"So you say, and I do read a book or two given all the time on my hands. I know what that fancy word means."

"Tell me, Walter, if I may, what do you live on?"

"I thought you knew everything about me?"

"I do, but I want to hear you tell it."

"Well, me and Rosy, we pan up yonder on the mountain for gold. We've found a pocket or two. Last find might take us through the rest of our days."

"I see. And…those necessities?"

"We don't like it, but me and Rosy was about to visit that little village below. I get water and supplies there. "

"Don't you have any human friends?"

"I know a feller or two in town, not exactly friends, but where I get my supplies. Don't hurt to be cordial. But then, you know, I've given up on friendships and trusting people a long time ago."

"That's what makes you interesting," said the Devil, and then he flashed that awful smile.

The curtain on the window abruptly opened, and through it streamed white light. Walter Miller turned and froze in position, put in that state by the entity that entered the cabin with the flood of light.

"What are you doing here?" began Satan, his human form shading his eyes with the back of his right forearm.

"You have broken our truce," came a sultry and pleasant voice. Behind it was the modulation of tremendous power.

"You have hidden this peculiar human from my knowledge," replied Satan, still shielding his yellow eyes.

"Yes and no," replied the voice from the sphere of light. "The human himself has done that."

"An interesting subject, neither good nor bad," replied Satan. "I was merely observing."

"Not true, you are intruding, and for that reason, I am here. You have broken the truce of noninterference. You are only able to judge after death, not before."

"But, I just stumbled upon this creature and…"

"And decided to interfere, perhaps influence. You know it is forbidden!"

Along with the sound of the gentle voice, the wind stopped, and dust gradually began to fall from the sky. Now exposed as an ugly, evil, and cadaverous form, the Devil suddenly transformed itself into wavering blackness. It hovered against the cabin door and as far away as possible from the concentration of light. The Devil squirmed in discomfort.

"Go back to your own realm!" thundered the white spirit. "But you should know this, you have tipped the scales in favor of this man."

There was a thundering clap, and the white spherical light flew through the window glass and straight upwards. Satan remained a smoke-like form that gradually sifted down into the dark cracks of the cabin floor to disappear into his own domain.

***

Walter Miller, blinked his eyes and stared out the open window. The wind and dust storm had stopped, and there was a bright sun shining down through a clear blue sky. Going outside, the old man slammed his cabin door shut.

"What in tarnation?" said the oldster out loud. "Last thing I remember was trying to harness Rosy to that cart."

Going about the task with practiced routine, Walter retrieved his horse from her lean-to and easily harnessed her. Going round to her head, he grabbed her bridle, pulled her close to him, and hugged her.

"Neeyyyy," replied Rosy in exchange, and then she bent her head and licked her owner's hand. "Come on, Rosy," said the old prospector. "We got a poke of gold to spend, a town to visit, and supplies to get. And I sure could do with a fresh cup of coffee, and I bet you would like a nice sweet apple or two!"

JOSHUA'S VOICE

The wagon train had started late from Independence, and previous trains and their stock had depleted the vegetation for miles on either side of the trail. These desperate travelers were without sufficient grass for their animals to graze. Worse, there was no rain, and the water holes and rivers had gone dry. A drought was upon the land, and they had traveled as far as they could go. When the water was depleted, under blazing heat, far out on the prairie, stock began to die. This was soon followed by the people. After tortuous days of thirst, man and beast lay down together and perished.

Joshua Jones was eight years old. His mother had just birthed a baby, and the child was stillborn. His father, using precious strength, buried the tiny infant in a shallow grave beside the trail and laid a stone for a marker. Joshua watched and listened to his mother and father. In rasping whispers, they spoke about their dreams and the regret of traveling with such an inexperienced wagon master. Joshua forced himself over the side and out of the wagon. He lay in the hot shade under it and heard his mother and father gasping for air.

Hours later, the boy heard his father's whispering voice. "Son, son…"

The child weakly climbed up and forced himself to enter that wagon where lay his mother and father side-by-side. Death had its distinct odor, and it was all Joshua could do to look at his mother. There was no moisture for tears, and the sob caught in his throat.

"Joshua," whispered the dying man. "Take this, use it sparingly, and walk away from here."

His father shoved a canteen towards his son. Then his hand dropped, and there was no other movement or sound, not even of his father's breathing. When the child reached for the canteen, he found it nearly full.

Every day his parents had given him a small drink of water, their water. But what courage, what love, what willpower, had it taken for them to save it all for their son? Again the child's sob choked him. The boy took the canteen, tugged a blanket over his parents, and then slid down from the wagon. Looking back once, Joshua did as his father had told him and started walking. He took the trail west, and as he passed other wagons, he saw nothing but death—dead horses, dead oxen, dead cattle, and dead people. The smell of death was everywhere. Animals, men, women, and children lay on the ground in various postures. There were buzzards and coyotes. It was more than any eight-year-old should have to witness.

Joshua walked for days until the canteen was empty. Then he, too, lay beside the trail, exhausted, hungry, and thirsty beyond measure—almost delirious. He hardly had the strength to scare away the vultures as they hovered.

Through his hazy thoughts, came a voice.

"Why do you lie beside the road," asked the voice, "when there is water up the trail?"

"Where?" asked Joshua through parched lips.

"Come, arise, and you shall find it yourself. All one needs is to have faith."

"Where are you? Who are you?"

"Waste no breath," said the voice. "Arise and go forward."

Using the last of his strength, Joshua managed to stumble to his feet. The voice stayed with him and encouraged him on.

"Just a few more steps, and you shall find it," said the voice.

It was much more than a few steps. It was nearly a mile—a mile that the boy would never have made on his own. Each time he staggered, the voice encouraged the youth. Each time he thought he could go no further, each time he fell down and cut his knees, the voice told him water was only a short distance away.

When there was no more strength left in the boy, he fell once more, and this time it was into a pool of water. Joshua lay in the cool wetness and, with weak arms, held his head up so he could drink. Water burned down his parched throat and into his belly, and it was only the beginning of quenching his thirst. The boy finally crawled out from the pool and rolled on his back beside the water. The sun and dry air pulled moisture from his wet and torn clothes. Exhausted, the child slept.

It was the heat on Joshua's face that made him awaken.

Opening his eyes, he could see that in this place, it had rained, and tiny green shoots of grass were coming out of the hard ground turning the nearby landscape bright green. The pool of water before him was shallow and clear. Immediately, Joshua knelt and drank his fill again. When he was finished, he crawled back to a jumble of rocks and into the shade.

"Ever since your people have come to this land, it seems there has been nothing but suffering, pain, and death."

Joshua sat up attentively.

"Who are you? Where are you?"

"You repeat yourself. I am what I am."

"But I can't see you. Show yourself."

"I will not."

"How come I cannot see you?"

"I wish it so."

"Then, please," asked Joshua, "tell me how you come to be here."

"I was created long ago by He who made all you see. Created and left alone."

"Are you GOD?" asked the boy.

"Hardly."

"Are you the Devil?"

"That may be closer to the truth than what I desire," said the voice. "Let us say, I am a spirit left neither in Heaven nor in Hell."

"No matter who you are, sir," said Joshua, "I do not want to be ungrateful. Thank you for saving my life."

"Spoken like a gentleman," responded the voice. "And, very eloquent for one of your age."

"Ma said I was smart. She used to read…"

Remembering his parents, the pain of loss, of remorse, and of their sacrifice, gripped him, and the boy choked with sadness.

"You cry most for your mother or your father?" asked the voice curiously.

"For them both," answered the boy, once he gained his composure.

"You were saying," said the voice, "that your mother read…"

"Yes, mother read to me a lot—from the Bible every day, and in the evenings she would read others like Irving, Twain…"

"A literate man, err, boy. I know of those authors. Even if I am isolated here, from time to time, I do absorb what is happening in this world."

"Do you have a name I can call you by?" asked Joshua.

"To give it means to…no…no name other…than to call me as you will."

"You said something to me," said the boy. "Something about…ever since people came here, there has been…"

"Suffering, pain, and death."

"What do you mean?"

"Perhaps it was a bit harsh for me to refer to your lineage, but it is nevertheless true. Since the Conquistadores came… you do know of the Conquistadores, do you not?"

"No, sir, I don't," answered the lad.

"They were Spanish and came from Europe. As I was saying, after they arrived the struggle for good and bad tilted, and with the coming of the European white, evil has seemed to prevail upon the Western Plains."

"But I am not Spanish," replied Joshua.

"No," said the voice. "You are not, but you are of European stock."

"What do you mean, the white has brought evil?" asked Joshua. "I don't think I'm evil."

"Enough of life history," said the voice. "I have disturbed the force of nature and taken it upon myself to save your life. Why, I don't know. For centuries now, I have remained neutral, and you came along, and I violated my own neutrality. Perhaps, I was lonely."

"Will you be punished for saving me?"

"Possibly, but what is worse is that my neutrality is momentarily gone, and I may be noticed by both forces. But enough of this talk. I reveal too much, and you, my curious young friend, are hungry. Since I saved you, I suppose it is incumbent upon me to make you as comfortable as possible. Now take up that stick beside you, walk forward, and do as I say. There is a rattlesnake sunning itself in the distance, do what I tell you, and you will come to no harm."

***

Several times while sleeping, Joshua dreamed of his parents. He heard his mother calling him to live, and to trust the being that had come to him. He remembered, too, the many discussions that took place as they sat before the campfire. Father had talked about the Indians and their belief in the spirit world. The preacher believed in angels and devils. So why, thought Joshua, should it not be so that a spirit, all alone in this world, existed in the wild frontier of the West?

It was blind trust that enabled him to survive. With the help of the voice, the child found food and was instructed on how to build a fire. Later, he learned how to find the right rock to make flake knives, shape a bow and arrow, kill deer, and tan hides. A cave became shelter, and while the boy learned to live from the land, the Spirit talked to him and shared knowledge of the world.

Still, in the long evenings when stars flickered like hundreds of tiny lanterns and coyotes called across the prairie and others answered, a great sadness engulfed the boy, and he fought hard to keep tears from flowing.

The Spirit recognized that the companionship of a voice was not enough. The boy needed touch and warmth of another living being. The child was lonely, and to fill that loneliness, Joshua was taken to a small cave along a dry river bed.

"Go inside," instructed the voice. "You will find in there a wolf pup. A mountain lion has killed its family, and it is like you, a sole survivor."

Joshua did as instructed and came out carrying the furry pup. The animal was afraid, and it growled and bit. The boy had to hold it up by the scruff of its neck.

"Be still, little beast," said the voice in a soothing tone.

Joshua held the pup before him, and the four-legged creature stopped struggling.

"He is hungry, afraid, and lonely. If you care for and protect him, he will protect you. Do him no harm, and he will be your friend for life."

"What will I call him?" asked Joshua.

"As you will," said the Spirit.

"Since he is a wolf, I shall call him Wolf."

"A good strong name for such a male creature," replied the voice.

Joshua took the wolf back to his cave. Within a few months, Wolf grew large and strong, and everywhere Joshua went, Wolf was beside him. As family, the two hunted together, ate together, played together, and slept close, sharing each other's warmth in the coolness of the cave. And the sadness and loneliness that Joshua had once felt, no longer haunted him. With the guidance of the voice and the companionship of Wolf, Joshua became happy. The lad actually reveled in the existence he led. He and Wolf grew strong, living a hunter's life upon the open plain.

***

As the boy grew, he became more inquisitive.

"Before," said Joshua, "that first day when we were at the pool of water, and you saved my life, I awoke, and you were beginning to tell me how the white man brought evil to this land. Several times I have asked you about it, and each time you have changed the subject. Now I ask again. What did you mean?"

"You forget nothing, do you?" commented the Spirit. "I believe I have said too much to you already. Someday, when you leave this place, I must make sure that you will not remember much of what we spoke."

"You mean you will leave me?"

"No, it is the other way around. Some day you will

leave me for people. And you must know, I cannot be among others of your kind."

"Why not?"

"Always there is another question from you, young man. Accept what I am saying. To talk to an innocent like you and tempt fate is one thing, to interfere with other mortals would mean the end of my existence."

"I am sorry that it is so," said Joshua.

"A very mature answer."

"Now tell me why whites have brought evil to this land."

The voice sighed, and it was some time before it replied.

"I will explain this once, and you must not interrupt, and then we shall never speak of it again. Do you agree?"

"I agree," said Joshua.

"Ever since the angel Lucifer was cast from Heaven, no human was ever safe from committing sin," began the voice. "Lucifer was the wisest, most perfect creature God ever made. Yet Lucifer wanted more, he wanted to become like God himself, and therefore he was cast out. But then, you know about this from the Bible and the teachings of your mother. Also, you know of the constant struggle between good and evil. In the beginning, here in this country, it was a balanced struggle, until…but then I get ahead of myself.

Here is a mystical place, created by God, with mountains, vast distances, dry and arid, that stretches for thousands of miles. I believe it is beauty unsurpassed, and that is why I stay. For the moment, much of this beauty remains unbound and unfettered by the touch of man. Sixty million buffalo, a gift from God that seems endless and boundless, roam freely in search of prairie grass—the largest creation of animals God ever placed upon this earth.

Storm, drought, and heat are natural kin to the Devil, and this place God created, unwittingly became a favorite for the dark one. Satan himself came to walk the dry desert land and luxuriate in the desolate heat—a land so favored by him, only strong plants and animals, and stronger men can survive.

In this West, Satan and God continue their primordial contest of good and evil—a contest that remained a balanced struggle, until the Conquistadores came."

At the word Conquistadores, Joshua opened his mouth to speak, but a sharp hiss from the voice and the boy remembered his promise and remained silent.

"With the coming of the Spanish, everything began to change, and with each advance into the West, nature began to change as well. The invaders brought disease, guns, and steel. In search of gold, they came to fight and pillage. On great ships, they transported their cattle and their horses, which enabled them to travel far. And with them came their priests and their interpretation of religion that still allowed them to enslave, to torture, to conquer in the name of their God. Their diseases alone killed millions of Indians—disease they spread on purpose as well as by accident."

The voice became low and deadly; anger emanated throughout the cave casting a chill over boy and wolf. Joshua shivered and wrapped his arms tightly around Wolf's neck.

"With them, they also brought greed that would forever change the Americas—greed for gold, and greed for ownership of the land. With their destruction and enslavement of nations and tribes—with the invasion of the white man—Satan's power grew. Through this evil, God's benevolent message of love and redemption fell on deaf ears."

"And you know this to be true?" asked Joshua, forgetting his promise.

"I have lived it and seen it since the beginning of time."

"What will happen as more of us come west?" asked the boy.

"Extinction. Indian tribes will be wiped out, as many are now. Trees will be cut, forests will disappear, and animals will be decimated."

"And the buffalo?"

"Will become nearly extinct."

"I see why you hate the white man," said Joshua.

"I do not hate what GOD created, I am only sad that it is *free will* that cannot stop the taking of land that was once so wild and beautiful and untouched."

"What about the future?"

"It is better I not speak of it."

"But I would like to know."

"I will tell you, and when you leave me, I will make you forget. Someday, there will be too many people upon this western land, upon the earth. All that GOD created and made wonderful shall be used up and become extinct."

"Even man himself?" asked Joshua.

"And perhaps man himself," said the voice. "Now, we

shall speak no more of this."

***

For ten years, Joshua lived a separate life from humanity and had as his sole companions the Spirit and Wolf. Living off the land, Joshua became a plainsman of unparalleled skill, and with a bow and stone knife was able to live as well as any creature on earth. Nature provided and, with the wisdom of this ancient Spirit, Joshua fared better than most men.

That is not to say they were completely away from other humans. On occasion, boy and Wolf hid behind large boulders and observed Indian hunting parties and even entire villages. A fleeting ache crossed his thoughts as he saw people laughing and touching.

"Do not let them see you," warned the Spirit. "It would put you in danger."

So, the young man merely watched and learned the Indian's daily habits, and when they were gone, he remembered. There were also wagon trains that came in the spring and summer of the year, traveling along the trail on their way to Oregon and California. On occasion, from cover, Joshua spied upon soldiers and other travelers passing along the trail on horseback. But not once did Joshua ever speak directly with any of them, and this was by choice.

Then came a day when Joshua grew tall, his chest thickened, and hair began to form on his face. Boy had become man.

"I notice sadness in your voice today," said Joshua to

the Spirit.

"You sense my mood well."

"Whatever is the matter? Have I displeased you?"

"Today, you will be leaving me," answered the voice.

"Leaving? Why? Are you angry and sending me away?"

"You are a man now, and you must live your own life. Down below on the prairie is a lone wagon. In it are five people, a mother, father, and three of their children. Two are young, and the third is near your age. She is nineteen and will be a young woman of interest to you."

"Why do you tell me this?"

"Because you need to be with your own kind. I will instruct you today what steps to take. When you reach the wagon, you will no longer remember me or much of anything we have discussed in these few short years—very short years indeed, for a spirit such as myself."

"I don't want to go," said Joshua. "You have been my friend…"

"This family, they are in need. Their mules are worn out; they are lost and without food or water. You will help them, and you will go with them on to your future. I have intervened long enough."

"I have no choice, do I?" asked Joshua sadly.

"None."

Joshua was certain he saw something, and the shape looked to be of an ethereal, transparent bearded old man—one who was very frail and shrouded in a type of draping cloth that revealed little except eyes that shone. Then the image was gone.

"Today is a special day for Heaven and earth," continued

the Spirit. "It is the day to celebrate the birth of GOD's Son, Christ the Savior. What you call Christmas. Life is the gift I give to you and that family below. Go now, and when you get there, you will have all the skills needed to lead them to safety, food, and water."

***

Sadness engulfed Joshua. One time he stopped and called to his friend of so many years.

"Please don't make me do this. I would rather stay with you. I was…"

Something pushed Joshua on, and the closer he came to the plain, the less his mind worked, and then ahead, he saw the wagon. Four emaciated and worn-out mules stood in front of the conveyance with a gray canvas spread over iron hoops. As Joshua approached, his mind became foggier still, until all that remained was the memory of many passing years of survival, alone with Wolf, on the great prairie.

A young boy darted out from behind the wagon, and when he saw Joshua, he shouted.

"Father! Someone's coming!"

A man appeared and beside him, a young girl. Behind them came an older woman and a grown-up daughter. Joshua approached, carrying a parfleche draped over homemade buckskins, and in his hands a bow and quiver of arrows. Wolf walked beside him, wary and alert. As Joshua came nearer, he saw that the father held a rifle in his hands, and all eyes of the family were upon the stranger. Seeing that the young woman was quite attractive, Joshua strangely became concerned about his appearance. He knew that his clothes were less than clean. It had been some time since he had bathed, and he was discomforted.

"Hello there, stranger," called the man with the rifle. "Before you come closer, explain who you are? Mind you, I won't take kindly to you or that wolf makin' any fast moves."

"If I wanted to hurt anyone," said the young man, "I wouldn't have walked up on you. My name's Joshua, and this is Wolf. I am here to help. Wolf will behave as long as I say so."

"Where did you come from, lad? We didn't hear any horse, and we didn't know anyone was around these parts."

"I have no horse, and you are on Arapaho land. There's a party of them thirty miles distant. Suppose I help you get your wagon out of that sand trap and get you to water. From there, you can graze your mules and let them fatten up some before moving on."

Joshua walked right up to the family, and the mother and two youngsters stepped back. It was the young woman who went to stand by her father, the man still holding his rifle at the ready.

"Who are you, stranger?" asked the father once more. "You mean to tell me you're out here armed with only a bow, and you say you have no horse?"

"I've been living here since I was eight years old," said Joshua. "Fending for myself."

"That's a story I'd like to hear."

The father looked cautiously around to see if there were others about. Seeing no one, he put down his rifle.

"My name's Ferguson, Henry Ferguson, and that there is my wife Helen, and over there's Billy, Lila, and this young lady beside me is my daughter, Nellie."

"Pleased to make your acquaintance," responded Joshua, nodding his head. "Now, how about if we dig those wheels out of the sand. It's not safe to be down in the open like this."

"I reckon you know this country?" asked Henry Ferguson.

"Like the back of my hand. You dig that sand out while Billy and I go cut some brush. You wouldn't happen to have an ax?"

"I'll get it!" said Billy.

"Mighty obliged of you," said Ferguson. "We're stuck for sure. Out of water, low on supplies, lost…"

"We can talk later," replied Joshua, waving to him and then to Nellie, who hadn't taken her eyes off him since he arrived.

"Alright, alright. But you're a godsend, boy. And I sure would like to hear your story."

"And yours, sir," said Joshua. "Especially how you come to be out here on the prairie alone."

"I got the ax!" said Billy, hurrying from around the wagon.

Joshua took hold of the handle and walked away. Billy followed, and coming to a clump of growing salt bushes, Joshua began swinging and cutting brush. Years of labor out in the open gave Joshua strength. It wasn't long, and he had a large pile. Joshua loaded Billy's arms, and seeing this wasn't practical, removed the pile.

"Billy, suppose you carry the ax, and I'll haul the bushes."

Mr. Ferguson had dug sand away from all four wheels. Billy and Lila laid brush in front and behind each wheel while Joshua went to the front of the wagon and examined the mules. They appeared overused from being weeks on the trail. All four stood with heads drooping. Coming to the lead mules, Joshua grabbed hold of two bridles and pulled. They didn't budge.

"Looks like I'll have to take the whip to them," declared Ferguson.

"When's the last time these mules had water?" asked the young man.

"It's been two days. We ran out…"

"Unharness the animals," said Joshua. "Billy and I can lead them to water. I know a place up yonder. There's some grass they can graze on for a bit, and then we will bring them back."

"If you know where there's water," said the older man. "We could sure…"

"Give Billy some canteens, and we'll be back before late afternoon. I recommend you not light any fires, or draw attention to yourself," said Joshua.

"But we already made camp here for two days now…"

"All the more reason to water the mules, let them graze, and then drive out of here quick as you can."

In the afternoon, Joshua returned with Billy and the mules. It was evident the mother and father were arguing and much relieved to see their son and the stock. Refreshed, the animals pulled the wagon out of the sand trap on the first try. Driving further ahead, Ferguson stopped, and except for Billy and Joshua, the family got aboard. On foot, Joshua led the party to water. He told them to wait, and he would return after dark with meat.

True to his word, Joshua returned with venison wrapped in the hide. In the shelter of a group of boulders, he built a small fire and began cooking the meat on sticks. Mrs. Ferguson and Nellie came to help, and they seasoned the food, and when it was cooked and cooled, the six of them ate their fill.

"Forgive us, Lord," prayed Ferguson. "For eating first and thanking you afterward. But we've been mighty hungry and thirsty. We want to thank you for our deliverance and for bringing this lad to us on Christmas Day."

"Are you gonna help us through to Denver?" asked Billy.

"If you want me…and if your father…"

"Son," replied Mr. Ferguson. "We'd be mighty obliged."

"I'd sure like to know how you came to be out here all alone," said Joshua.

"A wagon wheel went broke, and the train held up for us to fix it," explained the father. "Then a wagon tongue busted, and they held up two days fixing that. And then another wheel busted, and the trainmaster said we were mighty unlucky. He asked us to fix it ourselves, and they would camp a might longer and wait for us to catch up. He lied. By the time we got the wheel on and traveled all day and all night and arrived at their camp, they were gone. We tried, but could never catch up. I'm afraid I took a wrong trail and tired out the mules; then, we got caught in that sand and..."

"It's a miracle Joshua found us," said Nellie, with a burst of enthusiasm. "And to think...on Christmas day."

Her younger brother laughed, and so did her parents.

Nellie turned red-faced, and Joshua was oblivious to what the humor was about.

"I think it will take a month to get to Denver," commented the young man. "We'll have to watch out for trouble. I can scout ahead on foot. And if necessary, we can hold up by day and travel by night. We might even meet up with another wagon train. Then you'll be safe for sure."

Stars shone overhead, coyotes howled in the distance, and an owl hooted.

"It turned out to be a right nice Christmas after all," said Mr. Ferguson.

"Might want to put the fire out," advised Joshua. "It's protected here, but still, light has a strange way of reflecting on the prairie, and we wouldn't want to attract any trouble."

"Then we'll turn in," said the father. "Nellie, can you find the spare blankets? Joshua, Billy, and the wolf can bed down under the wagon."

Joshua pulled fuel from the fire and then doused it with water. Something about being with this family felt natural, and he couldn't quite remember what it was. When Nellie brought him the blankets, their hands touched. It was not an unpleasant feeling to the young man, and when he looked up to catch the expression on Nellie's face, she smiled. Laying out the blankets under the wagon, Joshua realized that after seeing that smile from Nellie, there wasn't one thing that would keep him from guiding the Fergusons anywhere they wanted to go.

*1st Printing, *Six-Guns and Slay Bells: A Creepy Cowboy Christmas,* Western Fictioneers (Nov 2012)

THE DEVIL COMES CALLING

It was past midnight when I finally fell into a fit of sweaty and haunted sleep. Just like every night since the end of the war, the nightmares returned and, if anything, dream after dream seemed to become more vivid.

I awoke, and out of habit, I lit a lucifer and stared at the face hand of my silver timepiece. It was three on the dot. Outside I heard the wind picking up and instinctively knew this was no ordinary blow. I lay in bed, unable to sleep. Despite the coolness of the one-room cabin, I wiped sweat from my face.

"Oh, my poor head," I said out loud, rubbing my temples.

Eventually, I planted my bare feet on the rough wooden boards of the floor, sawn boards I had hauled from near Pueblo to this isolated place on the mountain. Actually, my ranch was built below the peaks on rising ground and was at ten thousand feet elevation. I chose it for its privacy and distance from any other neighbor. I had endless views. A couple miles directly below were the meandering cottonwoods and green fields where a river ran. Despite the beauty of the place, it brought me no peace.

I got dressed and stomped into boots. Certainly the wind would affect the draft, so I decided against placing logs in the hearth. I made a fire in the cookstove, heated the remains of yesterday's coffee, and poured a cup. Its first sip was strong and bit deep down in my stomach. The wind picked up, and dust began to filter through cracks. With each blow, smoke exuded from the stove. The fire burned out. With the increasing wind, it became colder inside the cabin. Because of the dust, I decided to get my mules into the shelter of the barn.

Wearing no hat, I put a kerchief over my nose and pushed open the door. Outside the wind was blowing harder. It whirled in circles and created dust devils. Dirt rose high into the air and blocked out stars and the moon. Hurrying to the corral, I led each mule into the barn, and with trouble, closed the heavy door.

"Mary, Pete, are you feelin' better now?"

Mary, standing in her own stall, snorted a bray of relief.

"Pete, I bet you're glad to get out of this accursed mess."

The mule brayed, "Hee-haw, hee-haw," and in usual stubbornness, kicked the stall gate.

"Well, Pete, that's gratitude for you."

With difficulty, I went outside and brought in two buckets of water for the mules. Then I gave them hay.

"I hope this holds you, my beauties. I'm going back to the cabin now."

Exiting from the back door of the barn, I worked my way around towards the house. By now, the wind was blowing so hard, I could barely stand. With difficulty, I managed to get into the cabin. Inside, dust was filtering everywhere. I would be lucky if the barn roof and cabin stayed put.

The howling wind was hard on the nerves. In March, sometimes the wind blew for weeks at a time. But this was a real storm, a bad one. To be out in it, meant risk from flying debris and pieces of dirt in eyes, mouth, and lungs. In this kind of storm, animals and people found shelter and stayed put.

Morning came and a hazy light shown through the window. I looked out a crack in the closed shutter and saw nothing but blowing dirt.

"What we need, Lord, is a gentle rain, not a dust storm. The Devil himself must delight in a blow like this."

The rushing wind made an incessant murmuring in my ears that sounded like far off voices. Occasionally, I caught glimpses of land beyond the barn or of a dull sun to be quickly blocked by swirling dust. The smacking dirt particles against the windows and boards of the cabin made a constant crackling sound. Then, from the open fireplace, among sifting and swirling ashes, I heard what sounded like a grieved groaning voice.

There was a loud cracking noise at the hearth, and I saw movement. At first, it was a wavering gray shape. It quickly darkened and expanded. A silhouette took the form of a human. A figure with yellow eyes, wearing a dark suit of clothes, stood before me. There was an acrid smell that came from him, and all I could do was stare.

"Well, don't be so surprised, Mr. Thomas Willow. You evoked my name and my work. Don't look so astonished that I stand before you. Although, brrrr, I must say you keep it cold in here. At least you could have greeted me with a fire. There's nothing like a good strong flame."

Saying that the fellow stood in the large open hearth and snapped his fingers. I jumped back as several logs from a nearby pile flew through the air, settled, and burst into flames. Immediately, there was a cloud of choking smoke from the fierce downdraft. Momentarily engulfed, the dark visitor snapped his fingers. The draft reversed itself and pulled the smoke and flames up through the chimney.

"That's why I didn't light a fire," I explained.

"You surprise me," said the entity stepping out of the flames and into the cabin's interior. "Most men are too befuddled to speak. But then, you were always one of my prized subjects."

"I can't say that I was expecting you, but at least this explains the storm."

"A strong wind makes my traveling easier. Since you moved away, I had some difficulty finding you."

"And you think GOD himself cannot see you?" I asked.

"We shall not use that name again!"

There was a thunderous sound, and for several moments the flames in the hearth rose and roared loudly.

"What do you want?" I asked, dreading, and already knowing the answer.

"Since you avoid man and me, I have come to tell you the dreams won't stop; they will only get worse."

"Until I take measures to stop them myself?"

"Pre-cise-ly."

The room heated quickly.

"It's too hot," I said.

"If you think that'sss hot…," the creature's voice hissed, and the sound was like the rattles of a snake.

The Devil laughed, and his yellow eyes widened in mirth, his open mouth a ghastly cavern.

"You amuse me, Thomas; I can hear your every thought and inclination. You and I both know why I am here. Why prolong your misery? I will get your soul sooner or later."

"Because of the men I killed?"

"Exactly, a sizeable sum, and all from a great distance."

"I was a soldier performing my duty."

"Ahhh, the soldier's excuse, but then no one asked you to become a sniper, did they?

"Then if it is to Hades I go? What's the hurry?"

"In your case, I am an impatient man."

I had a flashing inspiration, and an idea struck. My fear lessened.

"You wouldn't be here if there wasn't some way I could escape."

There was another loud crash, and instantly the flames in the hearth increased. The heat became unbearable. The dark apparition before me wavered and changed shape. The Devil grew taller. Its ugly visage turned a gleaming red. Towering over me, the angry figure pointed a finger and shouted.

"I warn you! The dreams will become so intense that you can no longer stand them! And I promise you—you will come to me by your own hand!"

The voice shook the tiny cabin. There was a deafening clap, and the Devil disappeared into the hearth. The flames died. A rushing downdraft of wind was frighteningly cold.

For seconds I stood in awed disbelief. It was as if the Devil was never there. Then I sniffed the air and in it lingered the stench of fire and brimstone. I knew that his presence had been no apparition.

For an hour I stood deep in thought before the small cookstove. I stoked its firebox with wood, and it threw off welcome heat. Again, I fixed myself coffee, holding the warm cup in my hands. The growing silence made me come out of my reverie. I walked to a window and opened a shutter.

The wind had almost completely stopped, and the sky was beginning to clear. I could see the gray and brown debris literally falling to earth. The sun began to shine brightly through a blue sky. Directly below me rolled endless prairie and a line of green trees along the river. I rushed to the front door, opened it, and stood upon the porch enjoying the views.

I went to the barn. Mary and Pete greeted me with welcome braying. Opening the wide barn door, I led them out into the corral. They scampered in a circle, and Mary came up to be petted. When I stroked her neck, she brayed loudly, "Hee-haw!"

"Old girl," I said. "Things are going to change around here. Tomorrow is Sunday. You and me are going to get up early and ride down to that little church near Pueblo. He didn't get me this time. I think I've got a second chance to change my ways."

MICHAEL'S JUDGMENT

An angel is not supposed to have conflict. Not with those who serve the upper realm and certainly not with other angels. Having been ordered to minister on earth as a human, Michael retained issues he carried back with him. And, no amount of spiritual reverence, discipline, or devout behavior could strip him of his past human instincts. Even angels struggled with right and wrong, good and evil, and Michael seemed to have more trouble with it than others of his kind.

The most recent conflict came when he was appointed to judge souls. Discord came over what was the correct way to handle the countless requests for forgiveness. An unprecedented number had lived violent and selfish lives only to, at the very last minute, beg for redemption. Michael, one of many judges, took the position that the decision of entrance should be made on the evidence. Specifically, how they had lived their lives, how many sins they had committed, and how much harm they had caused. If not one act of kindness in a human's life had been shown, yet at the last minute the person begged to be saved, Michael declined the dying petition. By what right did a sinner have to enter the Kingdom of Heaven with a disingenuous and last minute request? With each denial by Michael, these souls would have gone to the Devil. And, in the struggle between right and wrong, such actions would have empowered Satan even more. In each case, Michael was overruled, and these souls were saved.

The entire Kingdom of Heaven moved against Michael, and it was Divine Intervention that suggested he take time to reflect. And so it was that this angel was sent to earth to observe and seek enlightenment. Such an action had seldom ever occurred.

***

Michael's spirit flashed through space and time, and not knowing where he was heading, he prayed. He awoke lying on the ground in front of a cave. Standing up, he discovered he was garbed in rough clothing. Putting hand to chest, he felt a heartbeat and realized he was once again wearing the mortal coil of a human. Coming to this realization was a shock, and feeling weak, he sat upon a boulder. Breathing air, smelling the dry earth, feeling the wind upon his face were sensations he had nearly forgotten. Looking up, he saw a full moon and a brilliant display of stars.

Where am I? he thought. *Someplace hot and dry, but where? What do I do now? Am I to be human and relive a life? Must I, too, choose between right and wrong? Must I struggle to feed and clothe myself and find shelter? GOD, help me. I don't know if I am strong enough.*

Chaotic emotions welled up within him. Michael, for the first time in centuries, felt fear. Standing, staring up at the moon and stars, the former angel, clenched his fist and shouted to the heavens.

"Why, LORD? Why have you done this to me?"

How he got through the night, he barely remembered. All he had were the clothes on his back. Sometime in the early morning, the new body of the angel fell into anguished sleep. Eventually, the pain of lying on hard ground awoke him. The sun shone in Michael's face, and he put one hand over his eyes to block the light. His exposed skin felt hot from the intense rays. Rising with difficulty, his neck and back pained him. Michael walked towards the shade of the cave and the mountain before him. Once again, he sat on the rock from the night before. A riot of uncomfortable thoughts came to him, and he began to assess his situation.

"What do I do now?" he blurted out loud.

His mouth was dry, and his stomach rumbled. *Is there no end to this? Is being human such a struggle?*

Standing, the former angel went in search of water. He began to wonder if he had been sent to a dry place in an effort to bring a mortal death. Walking along the edge of the mountain, Michael came to a trickle of water coming from a crack in the stone. Kneeling, now realizing how fragile he was, he drank. The cooling liquid went down a parched throat and entered an empty stomach. It felt and tasted so very good. Having his fill, Michael rose, and somewhat fortified, looked to the blue sky above. Shielding his eyes from the sun, he squared his shoulders and shouted.

"I won't die! You just wait and see!"

***

Walking out of the Colorado wilderness, Michael took a ride with teamsters. Providing care for the animals in exchange for food, he traveled all the way to Nebraska, where he found work with the Union Pacific Railroad. He discovered the year was 1866. Securing a job as a hammer-wielder laying tracks, Michael learned just how hard and brutal life can be. For six months, he lived in squalid conditions, sleeping next to unwashed Irish humanity, desperate men, working for meager wages, toiling day after day. Often, water-borne diseases ravaged the men, dysentery was common, and the constant fare of boiled potatoes and meat was tiring and weakening. Six months was all Michael could take. He quit, just like hundreds of other track layers before him. When he left the job, he found himself somewhere along the Platte River.

Meeting a wagon driver hauling freight and befriending him, Michael caught a ride back to Nebraska City.

"What's your name, feller?" asked the teamster, "Mine's Sam Drake.

"Good to know you," said the tired track layer, reaching out and shaking the driver's hand. "I go by the name of Michael, ahhh, Michael Stone."

"If you don't mind me asking, what brings you way out here without supplies and on foot?"

"For the last six months, I've been a track layer for the Union Pacific."

"That explains a lot. I hear the work is hard and not worth the pay."

"It was a struggle. Worse was the lack of water and bad food."

"Darn," said Sam Drake. "What was it like living with them Irish?"

"Hard. The company didn't give us water to wash. Neither for our clothes or our bodies. When I could, I cleaned up. Got in trouble for that, several times."

"Now I ain't saying I scrub all that often," commented Sam, "but not to bathe, ever?"

"They kept telling us water was for drinking, not for washing."

"I interrupted, if you don't mind, and since we got all day, spin me a good yarn what it was like laying that iron," asked Sam.

"I'm not really good at..."

"Come on, Michael! Tell me how it was!"

"Well, as we crossed Indian land, there were times when they shot at us. Men quit or ran away, and often we had to do the work of two. During attacks, we sought shelter. They gave us rifles, and we fought back as best we could. Sometimes soldiers were with us and sometimes not."

"If it was that bad, how come you didn't quit earlier?"

"It wasn't in me, Sam. Besides, I needed the money."

"Didn't spend it on those jezebels and whiskey in those 'hell on wheels' camps?"

"No, Sam. I did not drink liquor or sleep with unclean women."

Sam Drake laughed. "You're an unusual fellow."

In the evening, the long line of freight wagons pulled into a circle, the mules were unhitched, watered and fed, and remained within the enclosure. Food was prepared, men ate, and then sat around a campfire. Each man held a rifle close by. From experience, the teamsters were always prepared and on the alert for attack from Indians or renegades. Most of the men went to sleep early, and that included Sam and Michael.

"Here's an extra bedroll, partner," said Sam. "You and me will sleep under the wagon."

In predawn, the teamsters were up and ate a hurried breakfast. They watered, fed, and harnessed the mules and were on their way as the sun began to rise in the East.

Michael, given his nature, remained reticent, and it was always Sam who pried him with questions.

"Darn!" laughed Sam Drake. "Sometimes, I wonder if you're human. Here we been traveling for miles, and you ain't had one drop of my whiskey, swore, or told a dirty yarn."

"I was taught I must live a clean life," replied Michael, looking at his new friend.

"Dang, if you ain't serious. What about shooting at them Indians?"

"I want to hurt no man. Those I shot, I did to stay alive. I am afraid my soul with have to bear the scar."

"I get it," said Sam. "You're religious. Your folks raised you with the Good Book."

"You might say that. Will that be a problem?"

"Not that I can see," said Sam, rolling his eyes and crossing his fingers. "Tell me, if you don't mind, just how much did them railroad people pay you?"

"A track layer got $35.00 a month—when they did pay. Sometimes it came irregular like, and some of the men got heated about that."

"I bet," replied Sam, "with all them women, liquor, and gambling wagons set up next to your camp."

Not having his inner thoughts revealed to another human in the hard months he worked for the railroad, Michael was amazed at what he shared with Sam. In their conversation, they got around to talking about having to work for and follow orders of tough bosses.

"For a nickel, I'd quit this here job," said Sam, "and work for myself."

"I've been thinking about that, too," responded Michael. "Maybe you and I could go into the freighting business?"

"That takes money, my friend."

"I've saved what I earned," replied Michael.

"I've got some put away," laughed Sam. "Only because I had no place to spend it."

The line of teamsters steered their heavy steel-wheeled company freight wagons into Nebraska City. Sam Drake drove his wagon to the warehouse, emptied the return freight, and quit his job. Both men purchased horses, a pack mule, and supplies. Together they headed back along the trail to Denver.

"All this time and you still ain't told me much about yourself, pard," commented Sam.

"What do you want to know?"

"Well, for one thing, where are you from?"

"I was born in the mountains," replied Michael Stone.

"Yes?"

"Not much to tell. When it was time, I left and found work on the railroad."

"That says a lot. Talkin' to you is like talkin' to a stone," replied Sam, and he laughed. "If'n you didn't notice, that was a joke, pard."

"I don't have much to say about myself. I've lived a quiet life, and I follow the teachings in the Bible," exclaimed Michael. "If you don't like it, then..."

"Heck, Michael, I believe everything you say! You keep me on the straight and narrow, and we'll do just fine. First time I ever had a partner I could trust."

As they rode along, Michael began to reevaluate the last few months. Working on the railroad was hard, but now his muscles and body were strong. The few fights he was forced into with the Irish, he won. Men, he discovered, respected strength. Heaven had given him a superior body, and they hadn't taken all of his memory. At six feet and two-hundred pounds, he had an advantage over other men.

"Sam," said Michael, riding over the flat Nebraska trail. "Stay honest, stick with me, and we'll be successful."

"You know what, pard? said Sam. "You're a strange fellow. But, I believe every word you say. Put it there."

Michael shook his friend's hand, and the strength of it made Sam wince.

***

Immediately after arriving in Denver, the two men purchased wagons and began hauling supplies. Their growth was hampered by the virtual monopoly of Russell, Majors, & Waddell. Their new company competed with freighters who brought in large wagon trains from Nebraska City and from Fort Leavenworth on the Missouri River. Denver could only exist from the goods they supplied.

Working from that growing city, the two friends expanded their business and hired more teamsters. For three years they labored long hours and continued to prosper. When Sam slipped into drink or chasing a fallen woman, or losing money to gambling, Michael was always there to bring him back to the straight and narrow.

In the process, under the quiet guidance of Michael Stone, he and Sam Drake became fairly wealthy. They hurried to earn their fortune before the rails came to Denver to end their business. In 1869, both men sold their freighting business at a profit.

At this point, they discussed their plans. Sam Drake, rich and full of himself, turned solely to gambling, drink, and fast women. Time and again, Michael warned him of his behavior and that it would come to no good end. Their last argument was their final break.

"Sam," said Michael. "If you will give up your drink, I will take you with me. I want to return to where I came from, homestead, and buy land. I'd like to settle there and raise cattle and horses. Live a quiet life."

"Blast it, Michael! That ain't for me! I don't want quiet. I want to have all the fun I can before I go."

"And what about the hereafter, Sam?"

"You going to give me that religious crap? I won't listen. Besides, I'm tired of all those people you helped through the years. Just how much money did you give away to those bums?"

"They weren't all bums, Sam. They were people down on their luck that needed a helping hand and a bit of kindness."

"See! I wonder how I put up with you all this time!"

"Living right is what got us where we are, Sam. If you keep on, you will lose all you've worked for."

"Man, I've already arranged to buy a bar, and I'm going to set up the fanciest drinking and gambling establishment in the West!"

"You mock me, Sam. I warn you, you better change your ways."

"I won't listen to you! I'm glad we're bustin' up."

The two former partners split, and Michael left Denver and headed south.

***

Michael felt great remorse at losing his best friend. He began to reflect. The former angel remembered the day he found himself in a living, breathing, human body. Such despair he had never felt before. His first thoughts that day were of fear, anger, and hate.

Riding south on his sturdy mustang, Michael Stone smiled. He had come a long way from that first day. A very long way. In fact, he took delight in being human. The tensing of his muscles and the endless motion of the magnificent beast below him gave great joy. He gloried in his pulsing heart and the air he breathed. It felt good to be alive. In some ways, this fragile body gave him even more pleasure than being an angel. He looked forward to what would come next.

***

Going back to the cave and the stone spring, Michael

began his last stand. It took a few years, but less time than what he thought to build up a ranch with thousands of acres and hundreds of steers. Here he would live the remainder of his life.

The town of Pueblo lay below his ranch. There he befriended the priest, Father Raverdy. It was through him, Michael was able to follow his religious beliefs and contribute to the community. Father Raverdy came to him often; there was always some cause, some family, some project that needed funds. As long as he was able, Michael gave.

Still, it was not as if problems did not arise on his ranch. Catamounts came to take calves, and they had to be removed. The same with wolves and packs of coyotes. Killing these magnificent animals, gave Michael no pleasure, but when it had to be done, he himself went with his crew to trap and shoot the predators.

Years went by, and Michael lived an exemplary life— one as good as any human on earth. But still, there was always more that needed to be done. As hard as he tried, he would never have enough money to help all those in need. There were the many poor Spanish families, the poor immigrants in the coal camps, and the homesteaders who suffered and died out on the dry prairie. And, sometimes Ute Indians came to ask for help and were never turned away. Michael hired many of them and acquired a loyal crew.

But no matter how hard he tried to make a good life for those around him, there were always challenges. Sometimes rustlers came to steal his cattle. To keep what he built up, Michael found it necessary to fight back. When the largest herd he had ever gathered was stolen, the rancher had no choice but to pick up guns and go after them with his men.

***

With the help of his Indian ranch hands, tracks were followed. The rustler's camp and the stolen cattle were found. It was ten miles from the ranch, over stony ground, and into an enclosed canyon. Two of Michael's men captured the outlaws' guard. Leaving their horses behind, the crew moved forward on foot. Michael, his foreman Chris, and eleven hands entered the canyon. They discovered several acres of rich grass where the cattle grazed. Under a mountain crag, a cabin lay with its chimney spewing smoke.

"There they are, boss," said Chris. "Probably drinking whiskey and playing cards."

"It'll be dark soon," said Michael. "I don't like this business. We'll spend the night and confront them in the morning."

"They'll wonder about the missing guard," warned Chris.

"Perhaps. If they send another, we'll capture him."

"It's going to be a long, cold night, boss," said the foreman.

"It goes with the job," replied Michael

The outlaws did send a man to relieve the guard. He was also captured, gagged, and tied. At some point, the thieves began calling out to the missing men. When no answer came, the light in the windows of the shack went out.

"They know we're here," said the foreman.

By now, it was pitch black.

"I don't want to kill anyone," said Michael. "In the morning, we'll give them a chance to give up."

"Alright, Sir," replied Chris, "but it'd be safer if we just filled the cabin full of holes."

"No killing," ordered the rancher.

***

At daybreak, the crew surrounded the cabin. Michael called to those inside.

"You have no escape! Throw your guns down and come out!"

"We won't be captured, and I'm not going to jail!" shouted someone from the shack.

The voice sounded familiar to the rancher, and he stood up. A rifle shot rang out, and Michael Stone fell. He was hit in the chest. Chris rushed to his side.

"Boss, I can't stop the bleeding. It looks bad."

"I thought I'd have more time," whispered Michael. "Listen, my legal papers are with the priest in Pueblo. I gave him the ranch. I hope you'll stay and help him run it."

"Don't talk about dying, boss."

"No one lives forever," said Michael.

"What about the rustlers?"

"Try to take them alive, if you can."

Michael held a kerchief to his wound, and blood welled up around it.

"I'll leave a hand, and we'll go get this here job done," said Chris.

Ignoring Michael's instructions, the foreman ordered his crew to begin firing at the cabin. They showed little mercy. A white flag was thrust out a shuttered window, and the shooting stopped.

Two rustlers walked out, hands in the air.

"Anyone else in there?" shouted Chris.

"They're shot up," was the response.

"You better be telling the truth. How many?"

"Five! Honest, we ain't lying."

The ranch crew descended on the cabin. Inside, some were dead, others gasping their last breaths. One called out.

"Who's in charge?"

"I am," replied Chris.

"Name's Sam Drake. Hard to talk. Michael Stone and me were pards. Can you bring him to me?"

"He's shot bad, and one of you did it. Why should I listen to you?"

"Go tell him my name."

Chris ran back to Michael.

"There's some feller says he knows you. Calls himself Sam Drake."

"Take me to him!"

"Boss, you shouldn't be moved…"

"Take me!"

Four hands lifted the rancher and carried him inside the cabin. They placed him in a sitting position next to the outlaw.

"Howdy, Michael," gasped Sam.

"You stole my cattle? Why?"

"I did," said Sam. He smiled and coughed up blood. "Hard to talk."

"If you have something to say, say it."

"We were good friends, but you never would stop that preachin'.

"Go on," said Michael.

"Got so I couldn't stand it. I was jealous. Just like you said, I lost it all."

"Was it worth it?" asked Michael, holding his chest.

"I won't lie. Was a wild ride. But right now, I gotta say, no."

"And?" asked Michael.

"I built up such a hate, I thought it fittin' to rob you. Reckon it wasn't a good idea."

"Is that all?"

"Will you help me, Michael? Is there a chance?"

"For what, salvation?"

"Yeah. I don't want to go to the wrong place."

"Why should I, Sam?"

"Cuz we were pards."

"No good to ask. You have to mean it."

Both men were losing blood and having difficulty talking.

"I do, I sure don't want to…"

"This day comes to all of us, Sam."

There was a long silence.

"Hurry," whispered Sam.

"Say this after me," instructed Michael. "Lord, forgive

me for my sinful life. Please save my soul."

Unable to breathe normally, Sam Drake mumbled out the words.

"Thank you," said Sam. "Will it help?"

"I don't know, my friend. It might."

"Sorry, pard," whispered Sam.

Michael patted his friend's shoulder. A few minutes of painful breathing, and both men died.

***

The ranch crew buried the outlaws near the cabin. Michael's body was wrapped in a bedroll and put over a saddle. They drove the cattle through the canyon and down to the ranch. From there, Michael was taken to the church.

Father Raverdy and Chris talked about the rancher's wishes. The foreman and the men agreed to stay on. The day of the funeral, the church was crowded with all those Michael Stone had helped through the years.

***

The two ascended together, and Samuel Drake was to be judged separately.

As a human, Michael had forgotten the beauty and the endless space of the universe. Galaxies spread out before him. Burning suns expanded into blackness, the heavens filled with countless varieties of planets and stars. The power of the Creator was beyond comprehension.

A divine voice spoke to the spirit of Michael. Angels gathered round his essence to witness what was to transpire.

"Michael, it seems you have been taught a lesson—one

we sent you to learn on your own."

There was no response from the one being judged.

"Speak, Michael," said the voice.

"Is it necessary?" asked the former angel. "Each of you know my thoughts."

"We want to hear it from you."

"I was wrong," said Michael. "Those who ask for forgiveness at the end of their life deserve redemption."

BILL POSEN AND THE DEVIL

It was spring, and the past floods along the Cucharas River left the ground fertile and moist. The lowland was the one place where a good vegetable garden would grow in this high desert country where water was sparse. Bill Posen, tall and already tanned dark by the endless sunlight, was turning up the soil along the river with a spade. He was moving along at a slow, steady pace, creating straight even rows. Stopping to take a break and to get a drink of water, the rancher, turned gardener, walked to his cedar post fence and picked up a canteen.

Coming down the road riding a wagon, Jake, the local gossip and town ne'er-do-well slowed his horse. Too late, Bill could not escape.

"Workin' on Sunday?"

"I wouldn't call this work, Jake. I call this pleasure. Nothing like eating fresh from the garden."

"Looks like work to me. Come to think of it, you're the only one I know bothers to put in a garden in this dry country."

"Oh, I don't know about that. There's plenty of folks who put in gardens."

"I reckon. Say, how come you don't come to church? Don't you want to see the traveling preacher in LaVeta? He puts on quite a show. All fire and brimstone."

"I saw and heard him once," replied Bill. "That was enough for me. With all that fire-breathing hate he let out made me think him more the Devil than a saint."

"Folks wouldn't like hearing that, Bill. I kind of like the show he puts on. Gets me blood going and thinkin', I might even try to take on more work. You wouldn't have any for me, would you?"

"Jake, like I said before, I need all the chopped firewood I can get."

"Bill, you know I got a bad back. Got somethin' else that's not so vigorous?"

"You could muck out my stable. I'd pay you two dollars. I'm a might behind on that."

"Like I said, Bill, I got a bad…"

"Alright, Jake. Got to get back to turning the soil. I plan on stringing off the rows and getting the seeds in the ground before dark."

"Folks will be mighty curious why you aren't at the revival meetin'."

"Jake, you can tell them for me, I'm a good Christian, and I'm not going to sit and hear that fellow stir up trouble."

"Suit yerself."

Jake slapped reins, his scrawny draft horse pulled his rickety wagon forward. Heels of run-down boots on the footboard, he lifted a grimy hat in deference and turned his wagon towards town.

Taking another drink from his canteen, the homesteader

went back to his garden. He leaned on his shovel and wiped sweat from his brow with a shirtsleeve.

"Lord," began the young man. "I don't want to bother you none, but that preacher that came to town, he says he's on your side, but I'm thinking the Devil's got a new approach. I hate it when he goes on about foreigners and coloreds. He said he once was Saul, and now he's reformed like Apostle Paul. I don't believe it. Protect the town, and make that imposter move along."

Bill went back to turning the river bottom soil. Not taking a break for lunch, he went on filling his empty belly with water, promising himself a good meal once the planting was done. The young rancher worked until dark and then returned to his cabin. Tired, but proud of his work, he ended up chewing on jerky and drinking a cup of hot coffee. Laying down, he fell asleep in his work clothes.

Waking up at six, he remembered going to sleep and then nothing more. For the first time since he took possession of his homestead, he'd neglected to feed his animals. Fully dressed, with his boots on, he rose, went to pitcher and basin, and washed as best he could. He took a long drink of water from a ladle in a bucket and then headed outside. The milk cow was mooing in great complaint.

"Sorry, Hattie, old girl," said Bill. "I fell asleep on the job."

Cleaning the cow's teats, he placed a stool down, set a bucket under the bulging udder, and began milking. The stream was strong and hissed into the pail with great force. For once, the milk cow stood still and did not move until the container was full. She mooed in relief. Bill led Hattie to her corral and tossed hay. Then he pumped water into a bucket and took it to her.

The chickens clucked and complained as he opened the door to the hen house and they squawked their way out. They had been closed in for protection. In the yard, he tossed them cracked corn. Going in the hen house, he gathered five eggs and set them aside for later. He removed two draft horses from the barn and fed them, along with two gelding mustangs, still in their corral. The horses snorted in protest at the neglect.

"Sorry, lads," said Bill. "Pete, Sam, neither one of you fat boys need complain too much. I feed and pamper you as it is. When's the last time I rode either one of you?"

Looking out at the larger corral that surrounded the pond, he saw six steers, a bull, and three cows. One of the cows was missing from the herd. Bill climbed up on a rail and saw the animal lying down near the pond. The cows were going to calf any day now, and he kept his small herd together, away from predators.

Bill looked out over his land with all the pride that was in him. He collected the eggs and went towards the cabin and fixed himself a big breakfast, then returned to his chores.

On Wednesday, needing food supplies, Bill saddled Pete and headed for La Veta. There he stopped at the general store and made his purchases. It was a gathering place for women in the area, and they were discussing the visiting preacher

"Oh," said one of the ladies. "He's so forceful and wonderfully dark and handsome."

"I'm going to ask him if he will stay," said another.

"We could raise money and build a church," said a third.

"Bill, what do you think of our new preacher?" asked the store owner.

"I don't have much use for him."

The group of ladies overheard, and some gasped, and all of them reacted with indignation.

"How's that, Bill?" asked the merchant.

"I heard him once. He wasn't teaching brotherly love. The moment he used the term 'greaser' ended it for me. I got up and left."

Several businessmen walked in, and they heard the last comment.

"Here, here," said the hotel owner. "We folks need a little fire and brimstone teaching. Who are you…"

"I'll not be supporting a preacher that teaches hate."

"Well…" he responded.

Again several ladies gasped, and the men cleared their throats.

"What do I owe?" asked Bill.

"The minister won't like what you're saying about him," said the merchant.

"You going to tell him what I said? That Saul fellow got you under his thumb this quickly? I hate to see where this is going."

"What do you mean?" asked the hotel owner.

"No good can come from a preacher who spouts hate against others."

"Bill Posen, a heap of folks will disagree with you, and

I'm one of them."

The crowd in the general store voiced agreement. Bill pulled coins from his pocket and paid his bill.

"No offense against you fine folks. You know I want to get along with everyone. I live here, too, but I stand with what I said."

Bill heard more gasps and comments of opposition as he went out the entrance of the general store.

Getting on his horse, he spoke to the animal, "Pete, maybe I should have kept my big mouth shut."

The rest of the week Bill Posen worked hard, and he took pride in his accomplishments. When Saturday came, there would be a dance in the little mining and ranching town of Red Wing. It was some miles away, but starting early, he would be there on time. Sally, his girl, would be waiting. He had talked to her father, and they had an understanding. As long as he grew his herd and made a small profit, Bill would be allowed to propose. On Friday evening, the night before the dance, Bill awoke to a terrific blast of thunder. It was midnight. Lightning struck near the cabin, and it actually shook. Sitting upright, he listened to the fading rumble, and then, again and again, thunder blasted and faded away. Flashes of lightning turned the one window in his bedroom into bright daylight and then back to pitch black.

The wind shook the cabin and increased in intensity, dust blew in every crack and crevice. Bill rose and looking out the window at the flashes of light, he could see dark and roiling clouds. Strangely, the expected rain did not come. Walking barefoot and in his long johns into the main room, he struck a match and was about to light a lantern. Then came a flash of light, a thunderous blast, and the front door flew open. Through it, a cloud of dark smoke billowed. The stink of death filled the cabin air. Before Bill could react, the match blew out, the door slammed shut, and the room was encased in inky blackness. From outside, the wind and thunder ended, and there came complete silence.

Groping for another lucifer to light the lantern, he felt the undeniable presence of something in the room. A strange smell actually increased in intensity. A veteran of the last conflict, little rattled Bill Posen, but this was something new, and he was frightened. Struggling, he lit a match, He put a flame to the wick and the cabin lit up. Bill made out a dark and menacing figure.

"Who are you?"

"I hear you've been making libelous comments about me in town."

Peering into the shadows, Bill tried to make out the intruder.

"Are…are you the preacher?"

"Hah!" laughed the dark figure. "I have your teeth chattering, do I? You better be scared, you have good reason to be."

The voice did sound something like that fire and brimstone fellow.

"Are you Saul?" asked Bill.

"Yesssssss," hissed the dark shadow, and then he stepped into the light.

Bill recognized the preacher, dressed in dark clothing. The pale firelight revealed ghastly features.

"You weren't invited here," said Bill, now building up a heat of anger at the forced intrusion.

"I go and come as I please, Bill Posen. And I have come to warn you that…"

"Get out!" shouted Bill.

There was a snap of fingers, and the lamp that was on the table next to Bill lit into flame. The same with a lamp over the fireplace, and another on a wall sconce.

Bill backed up and stared in fearful wonder.

"As you see, I am not your average preacher, Bill. I have come to give you the Word, and that word is, obey my commands!"

"Never!" replied Bill. "I see what you are now. Hard to believe the Devil has entered my home."

"It was your mouth that brought me here. You will cease speaking against me, or I will close it permanently!"

"Do what you will. I can't stop you."

"Of course you can't!" The tall, dark figure made an unearthly laugh. "You could never constrain me."

"I could pray."

The preacher moved further back into the shadows and laughed without mirth.

"Threaten me, and I will burn your place down around you."

"I can't prevent that, but the Lord can."

The Devil clapped his hands, and from outside, a bright light appeared. Bill looked out the window and saw the barn roof on fire. Running forward in anger, he pushed on the dark figure and felt intense heat. Not stopping, Bill shoved harder with no effect.

"Lord, help me," called the rancher, and the menacing presence stepped away.

Bill ran to the water trough, picked up a bucket, and raced towards the barn. The vile apparition came outside, emitted a ghastly laugh, and somehow the man tripped and fell, spilling the water. There was another loud clap, and the house roof instantly caught into flames.

"You have no right!" shouted Bill, rising to his feet.

"Now you've angered me. I am going to destroy your ranch and take your soul."

"With the help of God, you won't," yelled the rancher. "Lord! Protect me!"

A piercing white light erupted across the sky and lasted several seconds. The dark clouds turned gray. Lightning was followed by rolling thunder, then came great sheets of rain. The barn and house fires were instantly extinguished.

"Bind him, Lord! Cast the Devil out!" yelled Bill.

Again light flashed, and thunder rolled. "NO!" shrieked the dark figure raising a fist.

Bill Posen saw a stream of light strike the Devil. The impact was terrific. All that remained was a sulfurous stench.

"Thank you, Lord, for answering my prayers and saving the townsfolk."

Bill looked out over his land and smiled.

THE SLIPPING SOUL OF WILD BILL HICKOK

Jack McCall sauntered into Nuttal & Mann's Saloon, Deadwood, South Dakota.

"Damn you! Take that!"[1] he shouted, firing his .45.

Shot in the head from behind, James Butler Hickok slumped forward in his chair. Dead. Blood dripped down on the card table and onto the face cards that Wild Bill dropped—aces and eights.

Unnoticed by anyone, Hickok's black soul slipped from the chest of the dead man and momentarily floated to the ceiling of the saloon. Along with cigarette and cigar smoke, the dark mercurial substance twisted and turned in complaint and then drifted with the smoke out the front doors and onto the street. A stiff breeze caught the writhing soul and pushed it along. There was no chance for it to rise to heaven or to sink to the depths of hell. In the wind, Wild Bill Hickok's essence drifted across the street. A downdraft caught it and shoved it, scraping along, directly into the path of a stray dog. The cur sat hunched against

---

1 Actual words spoken by Jack McCall as he shot James Butler (Wild Bill) Hickok

a water trough. Hickok's soul slipped into the dog's body, and there it remained, trapped.

The mongrel was a coward, afraid of his own shadow, afraid of nature, of his own kind, and afraid of man. As an animal without a master, the dog lived on handouts. He begged for food rather than fend for himself. That changed when Wild Bill Hickok entered the body and mind of the dog. Instantly his cowardly behavior transformed.

Up from its haunches rose the hungry cur, and it bolted into a run through town. The dog crossed a bridge, turned off the road and down a path to a rivulet of water. The animal ran swiftly, breathing in the fresh air, following the scent of a rabbit.

At the last second, the rabbit bolted and hopped away as fast as its legs would carry him. It momentarily escaped, but in the prolonged chase, the dog gained. Jaws bit down on the neck of the hare. Both slid to a stop, and the mongrel jerked violently and snapped the neck of its prey. Then, in primordial hunger, the dog bit through fur and into the meat of the animal. Blood dripped from his jaws as the cur feasted over its first real kill.

Something changed the cowardly mongrel the instant the raw energy and wild spirit of Hickok entered the dog. For the first time in his life, the hound exulted in its natural strength and ability. For as long as the man's spirit remained, the mongrel would never again cower.

After devouring the rabbit, the satisfied animal licked its jaws, cleaning away excess blood. The successful hunter then retraced his steps back to town. No longer did the canine slink past horses, wagons, people, and stores. The beast proudly gloried in its strength, and it paraded down the street lifting paws and legs in an excess of energy. The dog grinned with newfound bravado, mouth open, sharp white teeth exposed, telling the world to beware.

The hound trotted along, turned abruptly at an alley, and followed its nose to the garbage cans behind the town restaurant. Smelling something savory, the fellow balanced on hindquarters, and with its front paws, turned over the garbage can. It fell with a clatter, and its lid came off. Immediately the animal thrust its snout in the round opening and scattered objects in search of a hunk of meat. Nose and tongue found the piece amongst the garbage and snapped down upon it. The animal extracted his head and body from the can and devoured the tasty morsel.

The cook, hearing the garbage can fall, came running out with a knife in hand to chase the nuisance away. Many times before, the same mongrel had reacted in a cowardly manner and scurried. So the cook came to an abrupt halt when the dog stepped forward, growling ferociously, and baring white fangs. Then the animal began to approach the plump man holding the knife. Again the beast snarled. This time the cook, feeling the dog was about to leap in attack, backed up, turned, and ran into the open kitchen door and slammed it shut.

"That fool dog has gone loco," complained the cook. "Maybe it's got the hydrophobia."

Giving one more growl, the dog stood its ground, and then turned and proceeded down the back alley.

Since Hickok's soul entered the dog, a struggle of consciousness took place. The cur fought to maintain dominance, but its struggle was a weak one. The man's essence, much stronger, gradually took possession of the mind of the animal. Hickok, getting used to his new circumstance, began to gain control.

Wasn't supposed to end up in this brute, thought Hickok. *Was supposed to go—up or down. That's for certain. Probably down, given the men I killed, the things I done.*

Hickok felt the strength of the animal's muscles, its powerful muzzle, its strong teeth. The beast was underfed and needed more food, but still, it was no weakling. There was power in this animal, and a keen sense of hearing and a stronger sense of smell. These were attributes the former gunfighter could use.

Together, man and beast trotted further down the alley until they came close to the schoolhouse. Boys' voices were shouting and arguing, and the dog came up to a circle of them. They were surrounding two youngsters that were fighting. Sitting on haunches, the animal watched and listened. An opening occurred between bodies, and a large boy was beating on a smaller one.

"Hit him!" screamed one boy.

"Punch him!" yelled another.

"Tear his head off!" shouted yet a third.

"You shrimp!" said the large boy. "This school ain't got no room for a kid like you! My Pa said your old man was nothin' but a picker."

"My Pa's dead," said the younger boy. "You have no…"

"Good riddance! He ain't never had no decent job and you Short's are nothin but beggars. Take this!"

The smaller lad, dressed in rags, his mouth dripping

blood, held up tiny hands in defense. The larger boy, twice as big, doubled his fists and socked the smaller one under the chin. The youth went down. Hickok, through the eyes of the dog, had seen and heard enough. The animal rose and began to snarl loudly. Boys turned and saw the bared teeth and dripping saliva of the hairy mongrel. They backed up, and the hound entered the circle. The bully kicked at the smaller boy, lying flat on his back. The big dog leaped forward and, with both front paws, struck the bully in the chest. The youth fell under the heavy weight of the dog.

"Get off me!" cried the young thug.

The animal, still snarling, placed its cold nose against the chin of the boy, and stared straight into the lad's eyes. A chill went through the boy as he saw an intelligence he could not understand. The dog bit down hard on the youth's right hand, and the pressure increased as the child screamed. Then the mongrel let go.

The group of boys scattered. The bully got to his feet, blood dripping from his hand.

"I'm going to tell my Pa about you, dog! He'll come with his rifle and shoot you down!" He turned and ran up the street.

The hurt child lay in the dirt. Tears of pain were running from the boy's eyes, and a bruise was forming on his chin. The dog, no longer growling, went up to the youth and laid a front paw gently on the child's chest. Cautiously the boy rose to his knees and then to his feet.

"I don't know why, dog, but thanks."

Boy and animal looked at each other and then started walking in different directions.

The dog's nostrils picked up the scent of frying steak, and it ran down the alley and came up to the rear entrance of a house. There was a kitchen window open, and not only could the canine smell the delicious aroma, but it could also hear steak sizzling in the frying pan. It would not be long before the animal would have to eat again. Hickok's intelligence inside the mongrel made the big dog hesitate. They would make the wiser choice of not entering the home. At that point, Wild Bill felt the humility of being in a dog's body.

Across the alley, a cart and mule pulled up, a man and boy leading it. A lawman riding a horse and wearing a shining star on his chest, stopped and dismounted.

"From now on, Gonzales, I'll be taking a bigger cut."

"Señor Sheriff, my family, we need the money to eat, to pay the rent, please…"

"Whose idea was it to sell wood?" asked the Sheriff. "Who bought the mule and the cart to haul it with?"

"But Señor, you said you would only take half, and now you are taking almost everything I earn. What good is it for me to work if you take it all?"

"You're holding out on me, old man. You sold two cords of wood to the blacksmith this morning. Hand over the money."

"No, Señor! I bought food, I paid part of the rent, I have only…"

The mongrel dog sat and watched and listened to this exchange.

The Sheriff angrily grabbed Gonzales and began shaking him.

"Give the money you have or so help me, I won't be responsible for what I do to you, old man!"

"All I have is a few cents, Señor."

The Sheriff raised his right fist and swung it into Gonzales's belly. The woodcutter exhaled breath in an ugly and painful sound and bent over. His son, a skinny and barefooted lad, grabbed hold of the Sheriff's arm, preventing the lawman from slugging his father again. The Sheriff viciously back-handed the boy. Blood gushed from a broken nose, and the lad cried out in pain as he fell heavily onto the hard adobe ground.

The instinct of the dog and the outrage of the man inside of the animal reacted in unison. The canine grimaced and exposed a row of sharp teeth. Starting into a run, crossing the alley, the mongrel leaped up onto the Sheriff's chest. Balancing agilely, the cur closed his wide-open mouth onto the man's throat and bit down hard, tearing into soft flesh. The dog twisted its weight and held on as the lawman fell to the ground. Biting and tearing, the animal came away with a section of skin. It tasted bad, with the tang of iron.

The son rose to his feet and went to the assistance of his father, who had fallen to his knees. Both man and boy looked to the large canine and then to the Sheriff. The lawman breathed out his last. Then the mongrel dog turned and trotted up the alley.

"Why did the dog save us, father?" asked the woodcutter's son.

"Don't you see, Issadore. Heaven sent him to help. What else could it be?"

The dog felt tired and sought refuge. Hickok let the

animal walk up a high hill into a cemetery. Here was a favorite spot for the cur. The canine flopped down and rested its large head upon enormous paws. He instantly fell asleep, and now Hickok controlled all of the animal's senses.

It was then that the soul of James Butler Hickok was confronted by a spirit. It would never have been perceptible as long as the dog remained awake, but now that the animal slept, the man within could discern the wavering shape before him.

"You have given us an unexpected turn of events," the Spirit said.

The former gunman could only think a response.

It was not of my making, thought Hickok.

"Yes, we know. We've checked, and no one can recall these circumstances."

What will happen to me now? asked the soul of the man.

"If you voluntarily follow me, you will be taken to the usual place to be judged."

And if I don't?

"You are in the body of the animal. Under the circumstances, we have no power to remove you."

You don't?

"We do not. So long as you do good."

May I ask, where did you intend to take me?

"That is a question I am not at liberty to answer."

You mean, you won't. Let's see, thought Hickok in answer to the wavering spirit. *I either go with you to an uncertain fate, or I can remain in this mongrel beast, at least until it too expires. So long as I do good while in its body.*

"That, Mr. Hickok, seems to sum up the situation."

Then for the present, thought Wild Bill, *I will remain where I am.*

"Oh, dear. I am afraid this won't go well."

In *Heaven or Hell?*

"That is a disclosure I cannot make."

Then wish me happiness, replied Hickok. *For this cur and I plan on living a long life.*

"Oh dear," replied the Spirit again, and then its wavering form twisted and disappeared.

Wild Bill Hickok looked up at the cloudless blue sky, and then turned the sleeping dog's head and gazed down at the town of Deadwood. He felt the heat of warm blood pumping through the dog's body. The animal took in a great breath and then let it out slowly.

Man never lives forever, thought Wild Bill. *To live, and breathe in this body, is a small reprieve. Maybe I will have a second chance at redemption.*

THE DEVIL AND DONOVAN
FLETCHER

The great Western United States is a unique and different place. The lack of moisture makes the air clear and so transparent that the eye can see endless miles to far purple horizons. The ground baked by the heat becomes hard as flint. Ancient mountains loom large and dominate the land. The burning light of the sun travels across open prairies and escarpments, constantly transforming them into pastel colors and dark, twisting shapes. The West is a hard land, hard and sharp under the feet, with every plant and animal armed with thorns and teeth, doing their best to survive.

It was to this land that fourteen-year-old Donovan Fletcher, his grandfather, mother, father, and little sister came. From St. Louis and across the Mississippi on a barge, they floated their two wagons with everything they owned. Meeting a wagon train on the other side, they traveled onto the Oregon/California Trail. The trip was arduous, slow, hot, dusty, and endless. Some days they only made a few miles, and others as many as twenty. In good weather and bad, they traveled the two thousand miles. The train split at Fort Hall, and after five full months, the remainder of the wagons made it to Sacramento and to the Golden State—or so it was called.

The entire trip Donovan Fletcher was sorely used by his grandfather, his father, and even his mother. His sister, only age eight, was not asked to stand guard over the animals, the milch cow, and his father's horse, or bring or take the oxen for harness. Chief water-bearer and all-around hand, the lad was ordered constantly to fetch and carry. Perhaps more than most, the fourteen-year-old was tired of the trip and longed for it and the heavy labor to end. Donovan had nearly walked the entire way by foot and to keep his precious boots from falling apart, some of it while barefoot. His feelings toward parental authority were tenuous at best, and he couldn't wait to break away.

The taking of the South Pass over the Rocky Mountains was grueling, but the trail along the Truckee River and over the Sierra Nevada would never be forgotten. The Fletcher family was looking for the promise of a land of milk and honey. They were bone-weary of travel and decided their final destination would be San Francisco. Their incredible journey nearly completed, the two wagons traveled alone and followed the Sacramento River. Stopping for lunch, Donovan went to wash at the stream. Ready for the trail, his father called out to the young man. At that moment, they were confronted by heavily armed thieves bent on pillage and murder.

When the stentorian call came, "Shoot at will, boys," twelve armed men fired rifles at the father on horseback and the family on both wagons. With the first volley, the entire Fletcher clan was wiped out. The exception was Donovan, still in the brush next to the river. Startled by the gunshots, the youth bent over, ran to a clump of rocks, and climbed up. Remaining hidden, the young man looked down at the carnage below. The outlaws had thrown the bodies to the ground, and the filthy and ragged thieves were pilfering the dead. Others unharnessed the oxen to be sold or eaten and began searching the wagons.

There was gleeful and raucous laughter as the bearded renegades descended upon his family's possessions. Items were thrown out of the backs of wagons. There was the crash of furniture, his mother's favorite china, and then carefully packed trunks—gone through and tossed to the ground.

"Looky here," exclaimed one man standing over Donovan's grandfather's body. "A gold watch!"

The leader of the group shouted orders."Find the money box! These folks always have it hidden away. Tear up the floorboards, if you have to, but find it!"

Donavan looked on, careful to stay hidden. He was horrified at the actions of those below. Now he really felt guilty for all the animosity he had built up against his grandfather and parents. No matter what dark thoughts he had, they didn't deserve this. Once again, the leader, now holding a cap & ball revolver, screamed orders.

"Find that money box! And don't none of you hold out. When we get back to camp, each one of you is gonna empty pockets."

His father had built a storage area below the seat of the first wagon, and that was where the money was hidden. In it was two thousand dollars from the sale of animals and farm—all in gold and silver coins. Donovan watched as the canvas covers were pulled off the wagons. The axes were found, and men began chopping the wood apart, picking most likely places for the hidden money box. It didn't take long, and the seat of the first wagon was torn off. A metal box was discovered.

"Got it, boss," shouted a tall scarred outlaw.

"Don't you open it! Give it here!"

The box was heavy, and when the man threw it, it fell to the ground. Dented, its lid burst open, and some of the contents spilled.

"You darn, dim-witted fool!" shouted the leader.

Too late, the other outlaws saw the shining coins. Men leaped to grab at them. Two fought over a handful, and one drew a knife and stabbed the other in the throat. The dead outlaw fell. Blood spurted across the other thieves, as they fought. Then came a gunshot and the one with the bloody knife in his hand, fell dead.

"So help me, you curs!" shouted the leader. "Any other man who touches that coin, I'm gonna shoot through the heart. Jones! Grab that there box, fill it, and bring it to me. The rest of you louts, salvage what's worth havin'. Throw the bodies in the wagons, and don't forget to burn 'em."

As Donovan watched the looting and then burning of the wagons and bodies, something cold and merciless entered his heart. Having seen the leader and most of the outlaws clearly, he vowed to kill each one of them. All that he had been taught from the Bible and his parents was discarded. Hate and revenge consumed him.

Donovan watched as the remaining outlaws took what

was left. Standing on the rocks and looking up at the sky and then down at flames and smoke, he spoke in cold anger.

"GOD, you let this happen. As sure as I live and breathe, there's not gonna be a meaner or badder man than me. You just watch."

As the day waned and the sun sank, the lad went down to the burned wagons. Not all of the bodies were consumed by the fires, and it was a gruesome sight. Gritting his teeth, his first impulse was to bury the remains, but he had no shovel. The idea of using rocks came to him, but when he tried to lift his mother from one wagon, her arm came off. He rushed into the rocks to empty what remained in his stomach.

Eventually, Donovan remembered an argument between his father and grandfather. "Son, you can't be putting that money in such an obvious place. Be like me and build a box under the wagon."

The lad walked to the back axle of the second wagon. Using a stick, he dug for a metal box. Underneath hot ashes, the wood banged against metal. He pushed the box out from under the axle and testing its heat, lifted it up, and opened the lid. Inside a canvas bag was nearly five hundred dollars in coins. Also inside the box was a faded picture of his grandparents and a Philadelphia Deringer.

The pistol matched the one in Donovan's pocket. Attached to his wide leather belt were a powder horn, and a leather bag with caps and balls. Picking up the bag of coins and the Deringer, the lad stared at the faded tintype. He threw it and the metal box into the ashes. Taking one last look, fourteen-year-old Donovan walked away, no longer the child he once was.

The youth's transformation was like fire, and it consumed the brain of the young man. After a cold night with little sleep, Donovan got up and followed tracks. Staying hidden, he found the outlaw's hideout. It was a series of corrals, a spring, and one shack. He saw several killers moving about and decided for the moment to walk away.

Taking his time, the young man headed west. Eventually, he came to a makeshift building with a crude sign, saying **General Store**. Donovan hid his money, except for fifty dollars. Entering, he noted construction of wood timbers and buffalo hides, backing up to a hole dug into a hill. Two rough men stood before a crude wooden bar of boards over barrels, arguing with the owner. They eyed the young man and continued their banter. All three men were drinking from wooden cups.

"What you doing, boy?" asked the large, rough man behind the makeshift bar. "Get your old man; we don't serve runts here."

All three men laughed. Each one looking tough and mean.

Donovan put both hands in his pockets, grasping the loaded Deringers. The innocent and youthful-looking lad approached the men.

"I'm by myself, and I'll be purchasing food, supplies, and a rifle."

"Boy!" shouted the store owner. "What you be paying with?"

Again the men laughed.

"I have coin," replied Donovan.

"Let's see it," said the drunken proprietor.

"First, tell me how much for the rifle, powder, and a week's grub."

"Coin first, boy!"

Eyeing the men, the youth drew out two double eagles and put them on the boards. Then again, he placed both hands in his pockets and waited.

"Here now!" exclaimed one of the men. He wore a buffalo coat. Exposing yellow and brown teeth, he grinned viciously. "Where does a kid like you get gold coin!"

"Must be a thief!" said his partner.

"Yeah," agreed the store owner. "Suppose one of you boys go check outside. See if anyone's about."

It didn't take long for the one in the buffalo coat to go outside and return.

"The kid's by himself. No horse, neither."

"Well, just where do you come from, boy?" questioned the barkeep.

"You going to sell me the supplies or not?" asked the young man.

The way Donovan was feeling, he didn't care what happened next. In fact, he welcomed it.

"Well, boy!" shouted the store owner, staring at the coins. "You stole that gold, and we's gonna take it. Then we're gonna cut you in pieces and throw your baby carcass out back!"

"Try it," challenged Donovan.

The three men laughed hysterically. One began to wipe tears from his eyes. The two in front of the bar advanced.

Donovan pulled both pistols from his pockets.

"What you gonna do with them puny things?" growled the man in the buffalo coat.

"Protect myself."

Again the men laughed. The fellow in the coat lunged, and Donovan shot him in the heart. The brute gasped, backed up, and fell against the wooden boards of the bar, and it collapsed. The second tough shouted in surprise and raised a huge fist. The youth shot him in the head, and he fell. The proprietor bellowed.

"Why youse little brat! Them men were my pards!" The store owner turned and reached for a shotgun.

With the wooden bar gone, Donovan stepped forward. He drew his long Green River knife. With a quick thrust, the youth plunged the sharp blade into the man's chest.

"Why you...," gasped the crooked fellow. He slid to the ground and died.

The place became quiet, except for two kerosene lanterns sputtering weak flames.

Donovan looked around, surprised at his own abilities and calm demeanor. He reloaded his two pistols. Picking up the coins, the youth placed them in his pocket. Then he found a large pannier and began filling it. He took air tights and other supplies. Going to a display of used rifles along one wall, he selected a .52 caliber percussion carbine, bullets, and caps.

Outside, the young man removed a saddle from one of the dead men's horses and tied on the pannier. A second horse remained saddled and hitched to a post. Thinking it through, Donovan went back inside. Ransacking the place, he found a bit of money and some peppermint candy. Grabbing both lanterns, he threw them against store shelves and watched them burst into flames.

Going outside, he mounted one horse and taking the lead of the other, the young man headed back down the trail. A half-mile away, he heard explosions of gunpowder. There was satisfaction in the sound of it. Now he had a mission to accomplish and the supplies to do it.

Donovan retrieved his buried money. Following a game trail, he stopped a mile from the outlaw's camp. He led his packhorse and mount into a jumble of rock. Riding between granite walls, he discovered wet ground. Following it, he came to a small trickle of water that bled from solid stone and formed a pool. In the shelter of the boulders, he dismounted.

A good place to hide out, thought the young man, *until I decide how I'm going to do it.*

Donovan made camp. He found rope, made hobbles, and secured the horses. Opening an airtight, the young man ate a supper of cold beans. Then he spread out blankets, laid down, and slept like the dead.

It was late morning when he awoke. Startled, he sprang to his feet and banged his head against a low ledge of rock. The horses were grazing on green grass growing near the shallow pond. The water coming from the granite wall, gurgled gently as it trickled into the pool. One side of the narrow entrance between the large rocks was stuffed with brush. The horses had only one escape, and it was unlikely his refuge would be discovered.

His body betrayed him. Donovan, despite the events of

the last three days, found himself excruciatingly hungry. Fixing a meal, he took a chance and started a small fire. In haste, the lad heated his food and put the flames out. Filling his belly, he barely tasted the meal, but he did feel better. The water in the pool was drinkable but had a heavy alkaline taste. Cleaning up, he organized his possessions into a crevice in the rock and began to plan.

"Think, you fool!" he commanded himself. "What can I do against so many?"

For several days, Donovan stayed hidden. As hard as he tried, he could not think of anything that would work. Finally, he settled on going to their camp. Maybe he would come up with a plan there.

He rode near the outlaw's camp and hid his horse. Donovan climbed up a wall of rock and found a safe place to hide and watch. He counted fourteen men.

What can I do? One against fourteen? God or Devil, help me kill these men.

The thought barely escaped his mind when an eerie feeling came over the lad. It was getting dark, and a strong, hot wind suddenly blew straight from the south. It increased in intensity and didn't stop. Climbing down, he nearly lost handholds in the stiff breeze. Once on the ground, he found his way back to his horse and then to camp.

The first time Donovan Fletcher ever saw the desert, he recognized it as a magical and mystical place. Now that feeling came back and overwhelmed him.

He was much relieved to reach his hideout. Removing the saddle, he guided his horse into the narrow opening between the giant boulders. This time, he blocked the entrance as best he could with brush, and then found his bed. It was dark now, but the wind still blew, and dust filled the sky. There was a flash of lightning, and then thunder came in one loud, terrific crash. At that moment, the wind stopped, but dust still hung heavy in the air. From his blankets, Donovan saw what he thought was movement of a dark figure. Grasping his rifle, he arose and walked out of his shelter. It was inky black outside, and the dust made it darker.

"That will have no effect on me," said a low and malevolent voice, startling in its nearness.

"What...where...who are you?" managed Donovan. Consumed with hate and anger, the young man was not afraid. He spoke to the disembodied voice. He wanted to know. "Are you Devil or Angel?"

"Donovan," replied the being. "You asked for my help, and I am here."

"Show yourself!" demanded the lad.

There was a snap of fingers. The young man could suddenly see in the dark as if he had night vision like some animal. Before him was a figure in black clothing. Looking closer, he saw a thin, cadaverous man with piercing, yellow eyes.

"Can you see me now?"

"Yes," replied Donovan, "and I see you are no angel."

"I despise that word. So tell me, do you want to kill those men yourself? I can help."

"Would you do that?" asked the determined youth.

"It would be an honor, but I would not do the killing."

"No?"

"Something about rules between the two realms—there would be dispute. I would rather not have that."

"But you will help me?" asked Donovan.

"Cer-tain-ly," hissed the voice of the figure, suddenly disappearing back into velvet and silent darkness. Donovan lost his night vision.

"What do you suggest I do?" asked the youth.

"Come, young man. You have already killed. This time you will find it even easier. Follow me, and I will protect you as you snuff out their lives."

"And your reward, Sir?" asked Donovan, knowing full well what it was.

"Their souls, and yours, of course."

"I thought so."

"Are you having second thoughts? I came expressly at your…"

"No," replied the lad. "I just wanted to make it clear. I care nothing about myself. I want the leader of those men."

"Good!" said the voice, and then came a clapping sound.

Donovan found himself in the middle of the renegade's camp. The dark mist was gone. The moon was full over the land, the stars were out, and a slight breeze blew. How he got there, he did not know, but he was obviously transported by the dark figure.

"They are asleep," came the disembodied voice. "Go, use your knife, be silent, and kill them all."

Donovan drew his blade, the one he so carefully kept razor-sharp. Under the light of the moon, its bright rays casting shadows, the lad had no trouble seeing two sleeping guards near a small fire. The other outlaws lay asleep in their bedrolls. He counted thirteen. Across from the fire was a small shack. That would be where the leader slept—he and the stolen loot.

"Come, you are wasting time. Even my spells do not last long in bright moonlight."

Donovan was no longer a fourteen-year-old. At that moment, he was no longer human. His hatred for these monsters and what they had done to his family consumed him. It was not with lust to kill, but with a heart and mind full of pain that the determined youth moved forward to begin his ghastly work.

Donovan walked to a sleeping outlaw, bent down to slit his throat, and found he could not do it. The hand that held the knife shook with intent. The mind of the young man filled with rage and hate; still, he could not force himself to murder these sleeping killers. Perhaps it was his parent's teachings. Or perhaps it was the spell the Devil held over these men. How easy he made it for Donovan to end their lives. No matter how hard he tried, the young man could not will himself to murder.

"What's wrong with you?" hissed the Devil. "I bring you here; I make it easy for you, and you fail?"

"You cheat," whispered Donovan. "You make it too easy. I just can't..."

"You defy me in this way? When I offer my help?" roared the voice of darkness.

Ignoring the Devil's words, Donovan walked forward and entered the cabin. The head outlaw lay under the spell, snoring, sputtering, and breathing heavily. The light through the window showed the cruel, filthy face of the leader. Donovan hesitated. In his consuming anger, the young man held up his knife.

"Kill him!" ordered the Devil.

"No!" shouted Donovan. "He shall face me, and know who and why I am killing him!"

His voice was loud, and the outlaw awoke. Instantly he was on his feet.

"Who, what are you?" asked the man, staring and pointing at the blade. The renegade seemed to tremble with fear.

"You murdered my family, and now I am going to kill you," replied Donovan, in an emotionless tone.

"Then try!" shouted the outlaw, fear leaving him upon hearing the youthful voice.

From his clothing, the man produced a knife, and he lunged, cutting open a large gash across the lad's stomach. Without fear or hesitation, Donovan thrust with his knife, and it went home into the outlaw's heart. But with the last of the renegade's strength, he stuck his blade into the lad's chest. Both fell—Donovan with a smile of satisfaction on his face.

The Devil snapped his fingers, and the outlaw's soul slipped down into hell.

"You little fool! cursed the Devil. "You will cause me no end of trouble, but at least I got one."

A piercing light immediately shown down and around the outlaw's cabin. Trying to escape, the Devil was caught in it. Bright and translucent figures descended, and there was a faint ringing of a bell that resonated for some time. And then one of the angelic figures spoke in a melodious voice.

"You have taken advantage of this youth and his grief."

"In what way? He has already killed, and now he has done it again—and in revenge."

"We observed, we hoped, and we prayed this misfortune would not occur. You, Lucifer, have interfered and used your powers in a manner that is forbidden. You will not take this young man's soul."

"He would have killed…"

"Yes, but the fine point is you did not let him act on his own."

"And?" snarled the Devil.

"You know very well. This young man's soul goes with us, along with the rest of his family. Today, you have failed!"

The Prince of Darkness hissed like a snake, snapped his fingers, and disappeared in a haze of smoke. The spirits lifted both hands and arms, and the soul of Donovan Fletcher rose with the angels to disappear in an upward arc of light.

THE DEVIL TAKES A VACATION

It was the noise, the constant begging, the lying, the endless screaming, and the smells that drove the Devil from his domain. But it was never the heat, which was the one factor he could not live without. Even Satan needed a vacation once in a while. One where there was silence, space, and constant warmth to soothe the nerves of the entity of darkness. Such a place was the Great American West. Its very sands wreaked of death, bathed in the blood of countless massacred Indians and the largest herd of animals GOD ever placed on the planet—sixty million American Bison.

The vast dry deserts, bleak landscape, mountains, and scarred escarpments pleased the fallen angel. As purveyor of darkness whose business was taking the souls of humankind, he needed a rest. What better place than the Western lands, with such a rich history of killing and death?

Perplexed at the lessening number of souls coming to his domain, the Devil pondered. Inescapable in its truth, with each one taken, his power increased—and with each one lost, his power lessened.

"I MUST FIND A BETTER PLAN!" roared Satan. The air shook with the force of his loud exclamation, and the mountains rumbled.

Humans were born with sin upon their souls. Given the freedom of choice, so many followed the easy path of greed, hatred, and selfishness. But somehow, for the first time in centuries, the people were living more comfortably; prosperity was mellowing hearts. Religion and kindness were spreading. Instead of souls turning dark and black, the light was coming to them—the light of benevolence and spiritual redemption.

"I won't have it!" shouted Satan, and the wind blew hot across the land, stirring up dust devils and a mournful howl from a lone coyote.

Lucifer floated down on hard-baked adobe near the Mojave Desert and paced. For once, this barren land did not suit his inner spirit, and with a snap of fingers, he changed location to the high desert of Colorado. Standing on Badito Cone and looking down at the surrounding mountains and endless prairies, he took solace. Far below, a rare source of water in this parched land, the Huerfano River, ran its course into the desert. A dry, disturbing beauty, once a land filled with Plains Indians and great buffalo, stood virtually barren.

"That's better," exclaimed the Devil. "Greed and avarice did this. How can I return it? How many endless souls did I collect in those days? There must be more Custers, Shermans, and Sheridans! More of those corrupt and greedy politicians!"

The wind howled, and the earth trembled with the force

of his voice.

Sitting on a hot rock, even the Devil did not like the bright light of the sun in his eyes. It was setting, and soon the night would be perfectly warm and dry. In the dark he could think better.

A red-tailed hawk flew over, and its scream pierced the thoughts of the ruler of darkness. Satan smiled. The bird of prey's shriek pleased his heart. There were many such creatures made by GOD. Out of a crack in the rock, slithered one of his favorites, a green-hued timber rattler. The snake, its tongue dashing in and out, tasted and smelled the air. It came to the feet of the Devil, looked but could not see the unmoving figure before him. The rattler slithered forward to disappear after the prairie dog it was following.

"I must stir up these people. Who are they to enjoy the fruits of earth?" exclaimed the Devil. "I shall make this land hotter and cause rains and winds to destroy. Mud and rocks shall cover the ranches, kill the cattle, and starve the people. In this very place, my power will grow."

The hot wind blew, and more dust devils swirled across barren and sandy land.

***

Craig Revard, a former plainsman, turned rancher, wiped the sweat from his brow. This year was dryer, and the hay harvested along the river bottom was less.

"Please GOD, if you will listen to this sinner, let it rain. Give us another good year."

Deep in thought, the Devil was close enough to hear

the man's petition. Looking down, he saw him cutting hay with a scythe.

Instantly, this man's life history came to Lucifer.

"Well…this might be amusing."

Snapping fingers, the power of the Devil caused the timber rattler to change direction away from its prey. Of all the creatures on earth, this was the one the fallen angel had the most affinity with. Slithering in the opposite direction, it followed the command to go after the man. As the rancher worked away at his task, the snake undulated inexorably forward. Satan sat on the rock, watched, and smiled. It took hours for the reptile to reach the man. To the Devil, time was meaningless, and it seemed like seconds.

Stepping back from the swinging motion with the cutting swath of the scythe, Craig Revard stepped on the tail of the rattler, and the serpent struck. Fangs buried in the muscle of the rancher's right leg, above the boot top. The poison instantly entered a vein and began to circulate. Within a short time, the human fell, and once more, the snake, still present, struck the man's neck. The poison acted quickly, and within minutes his throat swelled, the rancher choked and died.

As the sun set, the dark entity sped forward and wavered above the corpse. It transformed into a cadaverous shape dressed in black. The snake slithered off. Satan grasped the soul of the transgressor and made sure it could not escape.

The sky lightened above Satan, and the dead man lying on the ground. From above, translucent forms descended. Four angels hovered over Satan and the body.

"Why are you here?" demanded the Devil.

"You have once again violated the rules."

"We all know this man's history," growled Satan. "Why he's killed thousands of buffalo and more Indians than most. His soul is dark with his crimes. We both know his attempt at living a cleaner life will not save him from his sins."

"Perhaps not," replied one of the floating angels. "But you are the direct cause of his death. You did not wait."

"Not this time! You are too late! I hold his soul in my hands, and you cannot follow me to my realm!"

"We will not allow this. Release his soul, or we will keep you here until you do."

The Devil's sinister laugh echoed across the plains. He defied the heavenly spirits and started a great storm. Through the night, the wind increased, the sky darkened, and clouds emitted great waves of lightning and thunder, followed by torrential rain. Water high up in the mountains ate at the dry soil until it turned into mud and rushed downhill. Gathering force, rocks, and giant boulders swept into arroyos. With the vast momentum, trees, mud, and boulders flowed down over the dead man's ranch. The cabin was engulfed. Cattle, horses, and corrals were swept away. An avalanche of material solidified ten feet deep over what was once open plains and prairie grass.

The body of Craig Revard was swept into the roaring river and floated downstream. More boulders, liquid mud, and trees rushed into the roiling river. Bridges were struck and collapsed. All along the banks of the river, rocks and trees were deposited, until the deluge flooded out onto the flat prairie below Huerfano Butte.

The storm of the Devil's making lasted all night. Not until the sun began to rise from the east and stretch across the land did it subside. He rose from his seat to look up at the four persistent angels. Satan laughed, and the mountains shook.

"I will take what is mine and leave now."

The Devil tried and found that all the snap of his fingers created was an ineffective hollow sound. He became angry and bellowed.

"YOU HAVE NO RIGHT!"

The very earth rumbled.

"Recognize that our power is greater," said one of the angels.

The melodious voice brought a gentle wind. The sun rose above the horizon. The heat of it began to dry the mud and moisture created by Lucifer's storm. Again the Devil snapped his fingers, his power suppressed by the cumulative strength of the angels. Growling, he stood up, and in defiance, shook his closed fist.

"So be it!" snarled the Prince of Darkness in resignation. "But you watch, I will make these Westerners suffer. When I do, they will choose the easy path, and I will have their souls."

This time, Satan's voice was weaker, and he opened his right fist. The soul of Craig Revard was released. It rose, and so did the four angels. Together they disappeared into the clear blue sky. The Devil stared in anger and then quickly looked away from the bright light of the sun.

Clapping his hands, the air vibrated like thunder. Sulfurous smoke billowed, and the furious Entity of

Darkness returned to his domain of eternal hopelessness and pain.

A BRIGHT NEW WESTERN DAY

I awoke and knew I had to take the train. Yet, hard as I tried, I couldn't recall where I was going or what I had to do once I arrived at my destination. Still, a force beyond my control compelled me to go down to the station.

There on the worn wooden platform, a bright light shone, and everything gleamed white and clean. It washed over people and objects and made them seem particularly interesting. The crowd waiting on the platform was dressed in their Sunday best—women in starched bonnets, their long, smooth dresses modestly brushing the tops of button-up shoes, men wearing shined boots, little girls in pinafores, and young boys in knee breeches, talking excitedly. There were people of all ages, from infants to ancients. Everyone appeared to be in a good mood.

The waiting steam engine and passenger cars were new and freshly washed. The black engine shone with bits of silver trim; its shiny windows gleamed. As more and more people gathered, the crowd filled the entire length of the platform.

I felt strange but too euphoric to ignore the compulsion to board the train.

Everyone smiled and laughed, and there was a hum of chatter as we began to step up into the cars. People were polite and gracious and waited patiently for others to take their seats. I stood at the end of the line and sat in the back of the last passenger car. The train was full.

The locomotive started with a hiss of steam, billowing smoke, and churning of wheels. Slowly the engine gained speed and chugged along. I was surprised at its smoothness. Of all the trains I had ridden in my life, none had started so effortlessly, or rolled so quietly down the long, gleaming rails.

It was such a beautiful day. That white light was intense, yet peaceful; it touched everything in such a calming manner. The buildings outside along the tracks looked bright and clean as if after a soft rain. When we came to the countryside, the green of trees, vegetation, and grass glinted with lusciousness. The plowed and unplowed fields reflected a variety of dark earth and colors that surprised me. Even the sky above was a restful powdery blue. The clouds hung fleecy white in billowing formations.

This was the world I was looking for, one of serenity. Everything my eyes touched was pleasant, peaceful, and tranquil. I had found the perfect day and time to travel west. I had never felt so completely relaxed and at ease. If this is what it is like to travel by train, then I should do it more often.

A little boy got away from his parents and came running down the aisle. He stopped and smiled up at my face with bright dark eyes. I nodded my head, put up my right hand, and he waved. His mother came and took hold, lifted him, and walked back to their seats. I turned and began to look out the window at the colorful landscape. This was going to be a happy and restful trip. I relaxed and fell into a deep sleep.

When I awoke, people were disembarking from the train. I sat quietly and watched them. I tried again to recall why I was here and for what purpose I took this trip. It was that lost moment when you suddenly awaken, and you can't remember where you are or what is transpiring. I concentrated and tried to recall, and nothing came to mind. I did not panic, though. When everyone had left the train, I stood and followed them out onto the platform.

That light was, if possible, even brighter, like nothing I had ever seen before. Now it was more intense, and I had to squint—but it was not painful. Everything had an aura around it and appeared fuzzy and unclear. The line of other passengers in front of me was long, and they filed off the platform and moved forward very slowly. I was not impatient, but I again began to wonder exactly the reason I was here. I was the very last in line when I came to the gates.

The people had disappeared, and there was whiteness all before me. Then I heard the voice and the question asked.

"Now tell us, sir, what have you done for others that we should let you enter here?"

Then it all came back. I tried to stop the bank robbery. I was dead.

I hesitated—all that killing and my time as Captain in The Great Conflict hung heavily over me.

The voice spoke again... this time softer, gentler, lovingly.

"Now tell us, sir, what have you done for others that we should let you enter here?"

Then I remembered, I had been a rancher, I had helped build a schoolhouse and the home for orphans. Maybe there was hope. Panic left me, I smiled, and began my answer...

BIG JIM, A TRIAL FOR
A LIVING SOUL

James Temple walked down the boardwalk towards Smitty's Restaurant. He had a real need for a good cup of coffee, a hearty breakfast, and some human conversation. Jim had sold and, as part of the contract, ran a herd of breeder cattle up to Wyoming. The trip back to Denver, he made on horseback and alone. Deadly tired of his own company and his own cooking, he couldn't wait for a good meal. Now that he had his life savings put together, he wanted to savor the moment. He would take a little time off before committing to his dream of buying a bigger ranch.

Big Jim stood six-feet tall. At thirty-five, the Westerner had seen his share of hard times. Having fended off Indian attacks in his youth, and taking the Union side in the war, he was hardly an innocent to death and killing. Perhaps it was the teaching of his parents and their faith that kept such experiences from hardening his heart.

So when others passed by a group of quarreling youths, the tall Westerner stopped to determine what was the matter. The foray took place on the boardwalk of Main Street. Jim, despite his great hunger, lingered to watch what the altercation was about. There were five boys, and four of them began calling names loudly and then thrashing the fifth, a painfully slim and raggedy-looking youth. The lad was overmatched and much smaller than the other boys. Despite his frailty, the child defended himself remarkably well, and he gave more than he got. The timing of his punches was better placed than that of the four bullies.

Having seen enough, Jim approached to help the boy. He was too late. One of the bullies shoved viciously from behind, and the lad landed in the street. He fell on his side in the dirt, and four large draft horses, pulling a wagon, were about to trample him. It appeared that nothing could save the youth from disaster. The four ruffians looked upon their victim's certain death. Being true to their type, they scattered and ran. Just as a large hoof was about the crush the child's face, the tall man leaped forward. He stepped into the street, reached out a long arm, and grabbed the boy by an ankle. Big Jim yanked with considerable energy. The lad was dragged back the length of his body, then brought up dangling upside down in mid-air. The horses and wagon pounded and rattled by, and dust rose up and covered both man and youngster.

"Put me down! Put me down!" cried the youth.

Big Jim smiled and held the lad's ankle with his right hand, noting the barely negligible weight of the child. The boy continued to holler, and in good-natured response, the rescuer righted his capture and gently set him upon his feet. One hand still retained hold of a small shoulder.

"Let me go, Mister!" complained the boy.

"Close call," replied Big Jim. "Those other lads have a

complaint against you?"

"Awww, they do that every day. They pick on me 'cause I don't have nothin'.'"

"I see," said Jim.

And he did, for the overalls of the barefooted boy were raggedy and patched as any garment the man had ever seen.

"Son, those boys play mighty rough. I'm afraid if I wasn't close, your noggin would be as flat as a pancake by now."

"I reckon..." replied the boy, and then he hung his head.

For November, and a brisk day, the lad was poorly dressed. Jim was sure he felt the youth shake, and he commented to the boy.

"Feelin' cold, are ya?"

"Aww, last week those jaspers took my jacket that Ma bought for me. I never told. But Mister, thanks for saving me. I thought I was a goner for sure. That hoof was mighty close, now that I think on it."

Jim let go of the youth's shoulder and saw the lad shiver from head to toe.

"What's your name, boy?"

"It's Tom Johnson, but everybody calls me Skip."

"Well, Skip," said the tall man. "I was headin' for Smitty's and a good meal. Since I saved your life and now have a particular interest, suppose you come along and join me."

The skinny youth looked up, and despite himself, involuntarily licked his lips and then hung his head.

"Ma says I'm not supposed to speak or go with

strangers."

"Alright then," replied the man, now bending low and putting out a massive hand to shake. "My name's Jim, and giving what went on here, I hardly think we be strangers."

Having never shaken hands with anyone, Skip hesitantly put out his narrow paw, and man and boy shook.

"Now, how about you and me put on a feed?" asked Big Jim.

Directly in front of them, a driver shouted, hooves pounded, and a wagon rattled. Then came a crack of a whip, and loud barking from a dog. Both boy and man saw a curly-haired mongrel skirt the hooves of the horses. Its barking caused the animals to side-step and miss the cur. The wagon jerked violently, and the angry driver shouted and used his whip once more, barely missing the dog.

"Charlie!" shouted the lad. "Here, boy! Come on, Charlie!"

"Fool dog!" shouted the driver of the wagon and then passed up the street.

"Come on, Charlie!" shouted the boy one more time, and the dog jumped up into his arms.

"Is he yours?" asked Big Jim.

Skip looked up.

"Charlie and me sort of adopted each other," replied the kid.

The tall Westerner smiled, put out a hand, and petted the animal.

"I'm mighty starved," said Jim. "Suppose you, me, and that dog of yours go down to the restaurant and see how much chuck we can put away."

"You mean you'd feed Charlie, too?" asked Skip.

"Sure, why not? If he's a friend of yours, it wouldn't be neighborly not to."

Again Skip looked up.

"If you put it that way, Mister Jim, I suppose it would be alright with Ma."

"How about if you call me Big Jim," said the tall man. "Everybody else does."

They sauntered down the walk, and then the rancher opened the restaurant door. There was a sudden rush of warm air, filled with the delicious odors of well-cooked food. One could smell fried onions, boiled potatoes, steak, and the aroma of coffee.

"Don't you be bringing that mutt in here!" shouted Smitty from behind the counter.

"It's me," called Big Jim. "The dogs with us, and if he causes trouble, I'll pay for it."

"Big Jim!" hollered Smitty.

The restaurant owner came running from behind the counter and up to the tall rancher. They shook hands. "Been a long time. Nearly three months. You back to settle?"

"I'm still looking for the right spread to buy."

"I kept my eye out like you asked me," said Smitty. "I sure do have something for you to look at. Suppose after I close tonight, you and me sit down over a beer at the hotel bar, and I'll tell you all about it."

"Deal," replied Big Jim, and again the two men shook hands.

"Now what'll you have," asked Smitty.

The boy and dog walked to a corner bench and table.

The mutt curled down at the boy's feet, looking up at the youth, tongue hanging. The restaurant owner frowned.

"Make it the works, Smitty," replied Big Jim. "I'm tired of the trail and my own cooking. Suppose we start with coffee, ham, eggs, steak, potatoes, and plenty of those fried onions. Three all around."

"The dog, too?" asked Smitty.

"Why sure, he's a pal of Skip, and any pard of his gets the same as me."

Coffee came first, and the boy helped himself. Jim drank his nearly as fast as Smitty could pour. When the food came, Skip and the dog, despite their small size, ate almost as much as the rancher.

When the meal was finished and paid for, Jim coaxed the boy and hound along the walk. They entered the General Store. Before they exited, the dog had a new collar and leash, and Skip was wearing new pants, a shirt, a denim jacket, socks, and boots.

"Gosh, Big Jim," exclaimed Skip. "What am I gonna say to Ma?"

"How about if you tell me where I can find her, and I'll explain it myself."

"Ma don't like me talking to strangers. She'd be mighty put out if you just…"

"We're pards, aren't we, Skip?"

"I reckon."

"I saved your life, didn't I?"

"You sure did."

"Now, in some places, saving a man's life means something. Almost as if that person is beholden. Don't you think?"

"You mean, I owe you?"

"Yes. Cause from now on, I got an interest in you and what happens. And doesn't that give me the right to talk to your mother and tell her all about it?"

"Maybe, but Ma will still be mighty displeased. She might take the strap to me."

"Now that's something to think on," replied Big Jim. "Alright, how about if I hold off on seeing your ma. But, at some point, I am going to have to look her up."

"Am I going to see you again?"

"Why sure, anytime you want."

"But how will I find you?"

"For the time being, I'm staying at the hotel. You can find me there or walking about town. When you have the notion, just come and look for me."

"That will be my pleasure," said Skip. The boy put out his hand, and the man bent down and shook it.

When the lad and dog departed, Big Jim went back to the restaurant to look up Smitty.

"Say," said the restaurant owner. "What's with that kid and the dog?"

"Just met them. That's why I came back in. You know anything about that boy?"

"Sure, his father was killed in a mining explosion. His Ma works as a cleaning lady at the hotel. From what I hear, they's barely scraping by. She and the boy live in an old shack at the edge of town."

"You know if he goes to school?"

"Nope," replied Smitty. "But if you wanted to find out,

you can visit the schoolmarm. She lives in a little place behind the schoolhouse. That's down on Fourth Street."

"Thanks, Smitty, I'll be seeing you tonight. Around seven?"

"I'll be there, but you got to buy the first beer!"

***

The school wasn't hard to find, and the teacher's little house wasn't difficult to locate either. It was around six o'clock at night when the rancher knocked. When he pounded on the door, he didn't know that the footsteps he had taken were going to forever change his life.

Big Jim Temple expected to find some old spinster lady with round-rim glasses, rumpled hair, and a sagging frame. The woman who answered was not what he imagined. What he saw was a well-shaped lady, in a practical gray dress, straw-blond hair framing a comely face. Jim was at a complete loss of words and was unable to speak.

In fact, his giant fist was still raised to knock louder, and he was caught with his mouth open. One couldn't call the schoolmarm beautiful because her nose was a bit too upturned, and her green eyes a bit too large for her slim face. Nevertheless, she was a looker by any man's standards. Where the outskirts of Denver ever found this vision of loveliness to teach school, was a question that echoed around in Big Jim's head.

"Yes?" asked the schoolmarm. "May I help you?"

All that he did was stare, arm and fist still raised, and mouth still open.

Now a woman of any age knows when she is being

examined and for what reason. And the longer Jim stood at the door dumbstruck and gazing upon perfection, the more amused the teacher became.

"Yes?" asked the young lady, yet again.

Big Jim just stared, totally mesmerized, his hand and arm slowly descending. His eyes searched her face, and his mouth formed into a silly grin.

"Perhaps if I fanned the door and gave you more air, would that help?" quipped the girl.

The cowboy continued to stare.

"You forget yourself, sir!" stated the young lady, now getting perturbed.

Finally, the realization of time and place struck Jim, and he quite suddenly came to himself.

"Oh...," stammered Big Jim. "Ah...what I mean to say is hello. No, I mean, I came here to talk to you."

"Yes?'

"Sorry, Miss. I forgot myself, I just didn't expect to see..."

Amused once more, the schoolmarm smiled.

"Hang it all," said Jim, taking a deep breath. "I'm not usually this tongue-tied. What I mean to say is that I came here about a boy. A slim little fellow by the name of Tom Johnson, but who calls himself Skip."

"Yes. I know the child," said the teacher. "Why are you asking?"

"I'm concerned about him."

"Unless you explain, I am not allowed to say more."

Then with an explosion of words, the rancher told her about the fight with the four boys, the wagon, the horses, and the close call with death.

"Go on," said the teacher.

"I forget myself," said the tall man. "My name's Jim… Jim Temple, most folks just call me Big Jim."

"I can see why," responded the young lady looking up. "My name's Hazel, Hazel Workman, and I hired on here last month. After Mrs. Jessup, the old schoolmarm became ill."

The rancher put out his right hand. Hazel extended hers and watched it become buried.

"Suppose we sit," said Hazel, pointing to a bench. "I would like to know what you think I can do."

Hazel sat down at one end of the bench, and Jim took the other.

"Let me start with this," explained the rancher. "I wanted to meet Skip's mother, and he wouldn't let me? Can you tell me why?"

"I can, but I do have to be careful what I say."

"I promise I won't compromise you," replied Big Jim.

"I was concerned about Skip missing school, so I went around to see his mother. Let me just say that the two of them are struggling."

"I want to help the boy," said Jim. "I think I can do that best through you. He's a likable little cuss."

"What do you have in mind?"

"I wanted to start by finding out who those four boys are who were picking on him."

"Yes?" asked Hazel. "What could you do about that?"

"They nearly killed the kid. For one thing, I could talk to their fathers."

"That might help," smiled Hazel.

"For another, I'll be buying a ranch soon, and I'll be needing someone to cook and keep house, and I figured…"

"That you might hire Skip's mother?"

"It was a thought. No boy should go without. That little scamp…why the clothes he was wearing were washed to rags. It was cold, and he was barefoot and without a jacket. He's likely to catch his death of…"

"It's very nice, or may I say unusual that you should want to help some child you hardly know."

"I saved his life, darn it! Don't I have a right to…"

Hazel laughed, and it was a warm and comforting sound.

"No need to make jest, Miss Workman," said Jim. "I know I might be making a fool of myself. But when I was young, there were people who looked out after me. Why can't I…"

"I think what you're planning is grand," responded the girl.

"Then you'll give me the names of the boys who…"

"I can't," replied Hazel. "It doesn't mean I don't want to, but it's against school policy. I would be fired."

"Don't want that, but how do I get…"

"I suggest you come when the students are leaving school, identify the boys, and follow them home. You do remember their faces?"

"Wouldn't forget the little bullies in a million years."

"Well then, problem solved."

"Not all of it," declared Big Jim. "I still need to speak to his mother."

"You'll have to work that out yourself. How can I put this? She's had a rough time, and doesn't trust anyone."

There was a momentary silence.

"But it is a shame he misses so much school," began Hazel. "If he applied himself, he could excel."

"I think the boy likes me," replied Big Jim. "Perhaps I can talk to him about it."

"That would be great! But both of them need so much help."

"Like I said, I'll be buying a ranch, and I'm not much of a housekeeper."

"Jim, I just met you, but what you plan on doing is wonderful."

"Don't say it, I've done nothing yet."

With that, Jim pulled out a watch and noted it was half-past six.

"I'm sorry, I have an appointment about locating a ranch. I appreciate your helping me with the lad. First chance I get, I'll talk to him about school. Tomorrow or the next day, I'll locate the bullies' fathers."

"I look forward to seeing you again. I'm sure together we will find a way to help Skip," replied Hazel.

They both rose from the bench and shook hands. Hazel looked up and smiled. Jim nodded his head and raised his fingers to his Stetson. Feeling her eyes on his back, he walked away. Her very presence had a profound effect, one he had never felt before.

For certain, thought Jim. *Every male in the county will be chasing after her. They'll have to be fast on their feet to catch up with me! Thank you, Lord, for letting me save that boy's life.*

***

"Thanks for the beer, Big Jim!" declared Smitty. "Now looky here, I narrowed down the search to exactly what you told me you wanted. I brought maps on two ranches. This one over here is ten miles out and is a pretty nice spread."

"What about water?" asked Jim.

"I'm getting to it, I'm getting to it! Be patient. You waited this long, let me tell you about both of these beauties."

"You went out and saw them?"

"Jim!" complained Smitty. "You put this in my hands. Now be quiet and hear me out!"

***

The next day, the rancher got up early and washed and dressed before sunup. He walked to the stable and found Smitty, yawning and sipping a cup of coffee. The restaurant owner was jawing with the hostler, and it was some time before they noticed Jim.

"You ready to go see those spreads?" asked Smitty.

"As ready as I'll ever be. Who you got looking after the restaurant?"

"I hired a lady a while back to fill in when I was sick or not feeling up to par. This ranch selling business is starting to take off. I'd rather work for the commissions."

"Why not do both, Smitty?" asked Jim.

They rode the trail south and traveled among squat

Ponderosa Pine. The first ranch the men visited had two springs, an intermittent stream, and plenty of catch ponds. The farmhouse, barns, and corrals were a run-down affair, and the price was high for ten thousand acres of deeded land.

The second place was another five miles out, and it butted up against some large hills and a small mountain. It had several springs, a little lake, and a wash that ran water from snowmelt. A large dam could be built, and an enormous amount of water retained. There were fifteen thousand acres and open range that could be used for cattle. What sold the place was the big barn, the quarters for the cowhands, and a large ranch house.

"How much?" Jim asked.

Smitty told him.

"That's top price, alright."

"It is. I searched a while until I found this place. It won't last long."

"Any wiggle room?" asked Big Jim.

"Afraid not."

"Alright, Smitty," said Jim. "Let's sign the papers and have the owner meet me at the bank."

"I figured you'd like this one. I've got the paperwork ready. All you have to do is sign and deposit the money in the owner's account. Is it like I said it was?"

"Smitty, you do good work."

***

Big Jim didn't get back into town until late. The next day he was near the school when the children let out. He watched the four bullies join up for their walk home. It was the tall, stocky kid that Jim wanted most. That was the one who had pushed Skip into the street and nearly got him killed. It was a simple walk down a couple blocks, and the largest youth pared off and went into a house. Jim noted it and then followed the other three. It didn't take long to mark off where all four boys lived.

The rancher decided to wait until supper time before knocking on doors. It was about five-thirty when he came to the first bully's house.

"What do ya want?" asked a burly man who answered the back door.

To Jim, the man looked like a miner. He held plenty of muscle and was stocky and thick around the chest. Despite the cool air, the man was shirtless.

"Howdy, folks call me Big Jim; I came here to talk to you about your son."

The man's face turned red.

"What about him?"

"On Saturday, about noon, your son and three boys picked on a frail little boy they call Skip.

"Yeah?"

"Your son pushed him into the street and almost got him killed. A horse nearly stomped the boy's head in."

"Mister, I don't know nothin' about it, and I raised my boy to fend for himself. So if you got any beef about it, you can go to..."

"Won't happen," replied Big Jim.

"Then, if you want trouble, you've come to the right place."

"I figured it would be like that. Like father, like son."

"What does that mean? You come to my house, take me away from my supper, and make wisecracks. Mister, I ought to knock your block off."

Big Jim stepped forward and smiled. "Suppose you try, you big dumb ox!"

Angry now, the burly man stepped off the porch, clenching fists. He bent his head and threw a right punch, followed by a wicked left. Jim blocked the first, sidestepped the second, and delivered a powerful right to the father's face. This was followed by a quick shove. The man tripped and went down.

Surprisingly, the stocky fellow jumped up and growled. He threw another right and left, and Jim simply backed up. The punches merely caught air. Jim thrust out a right arm, clenched his fist, and thumped the man on the top of his head. Stunned, the miner collapsed to the ground. Jim nudged the fighter with the toe of his right boot. He pressed down hard on the burly man's shoulder.

"That hurts, Mister," said the bully's father. "How come you got to come and pick on me?"

"Now suppose you stay down," said Big Jim. "You're no match for me, and neither is your son. Now, this is the way it's going to be. Your kid leaves Skip alone, or whatever your boy dishes out, I'll give to you twice fold."

"What gives you the right?" growled the father. "You ain't got no call to be bothering hard-working folk!"

"I came to ask polite like, to keep your brute of a boy from bullying a frail little kid. You wanted to fight instead. Next time, I won't be so gentle."

Big Jim applied more pressure with the toe of his boot on the man's shoulder.

"Alright! Alright!" responded the father. "I'll talk to Henry and make sure he don't do nothin' to..."

"The lad's name is Skip. You just remember. Whatever Henry does to him, I do to you."

Jim released his foot, and the man sat up. As the rancher began to walk away, the miner yelled at him.

"Maybe someone should take a gun to you. Mister, when you ain't lookin'."

Big Jim turned and walked several steps forward, bent down and grasped the man's shoulders. He squeezed hard with both hands and lifted up the fellow as if he was a lightweight. Jim held him in the air and shook him like a ragdoll. The man tried to resist the grasp but to no avail.

"Alright, tough guy," said Big Jim, holding the man in the air. "If you want gunplay, you can have it. Right now, or tomorrow, or any time you say. And you remember this. It'll be a fair fight, and I'll still put a bullet between your eyes and kill you dead. Now you think on that before threatening to dry-gulch me!"

"I didn't mean to, Mister," whined the father. "I'm no hand with guns, I was just plain mad and..."

The tall rancher let go, and the miner dropped to his feet. Jim stared down at him, and the father cowered and stepped back.

"Alright, alright!" said the man. "I'll do as you say. Henry won't bother that Skip no more."

"That's better," said Big Jim, and he stepped away.

The rancher made a visit to the other parents, all

merchants. Each father was upset in learning about his son's behavior. They agreed to stop the bullying.

***

The next week Jim took it easy. He slept in late, and every day went to Smitty's to eat and play a little poker. Twice in the afternoon, Skip and his dog Charlie came to visit, and both times the rancher purchased dinner. Despite Jim asking, the lad was hesitant to talk about his mother. Before leaving for the ranch, Jim set it up with Smitty that if Skip and his dog came to the restaurant, they would be fed.

Big Jim brought in his old hands and hired more. Cattle, horses, crew, and personal effects were moved from the old spread to the new. The smaller ranch was put up for sale. Well pleased with his purchase, he spent days in the saddle going over every acre.

Jim wrote a note to the schoolmarm. He simply stated he believed the bully problem was resolved. On the second Saturday in December, he planned on being in town, meeting Skip's mother, and then attending the Saturday night dance. Jim hoped they could meet at that time, and perhaps she would share a dance.

Her reply was on a decorative card.

Dear Jim,

I am in receipt of your letter. Indeed the life of Skip has greatly improved. He is better dressed, and I attribute that to your intervention. The four boys in question stay well away from Skip, and they no longer bother him.

I don't know what you said, but he attends school every day.

You must be very busy, indeed, with your new ranch. I look forward to seeing you. It would be my distinct pleasure to save several dances.

Sincerely,
Hazel Workman

***

Jim knocked on the door of the flimsy shack. It was an ugly ramshackle affair put together with mismatched boards. Rusted cans, smashed flat, covered the roof and holes in the sides of the building. Much of it was torn and shifting in the wind. He knocked again, this time with more force, and the makeshift door shook. It opened, and the woman Jim expected to see was not what he encountered. Skip's mother should be no older than forty. But in front of the rancher stood a tired old woman who looked sixty. Hazel had it right, Skip's mother looked like she had a hard life.

"What do you want, Mister?" growled the woman.

"Ma'am, I'm Jim Temple. I sent you a note that I would come calling today."

"Yeah, I got it," answered the mother, suspiciously. "You that fancy dude who's been trying to buy my son off?"

"You're wrong, Mrs. Johnson."

"So you know my name and everything about Skip and me, but I know nothin' 'bout you! How's come you're sticking your nose in…"

"Did your son tell you I saved his life?"

"Yeah, he mentioned it. Said those no-good boys about town were picking on him, and you came along and…"

"I'm glad he told you, Mrs. Johnson," interrupted Jim. "Now, if you save a life, that kind of gets a man involved. And besides, your son Skip is a right likable lad."

"He's a good boy," replied the mother, cautiously. "Most times, but that don't explain why you're so interested."

"That's why I'm here. Since I got to know Skip, I want what's best for him."

"I knew it! I told Skip you'd be coming around, sticking it in my face that I don't provide right for him, and you'd be wantin' to take him away from…"

"Not at all, Mrs. Johnson. Skip loves you and cares about you. He told me so himself. A boy deserves his mother."

"Then what do you want?"

"I want to offer you a job on my ranch. Room and board for you and the boy, and forty dollars a month. All I'm asking is for you to care for my house and help Cookie feed the crew."

Mrs. Johnson looked up at the big man and then turned and went back into the cabin. The door was left open, so the rancher stooped at the frame and followed her in. The place was a crude one-room affair. No amount of fixing could hide the dilapidated condition. The woman sat hunched over a wobbly board table, crying. Jim came near and stood next to her.

"I didn't mean to upset you, Ma'am," he said in as soft

a voice as he could manage.

"Skip told me you was a good man, but I just wouldn't believe it."

"It's going to be alright now, Mrs. Johnson. Together you and I can help raise that fine boy of yours. And there won't be any hardship on you. I'll see to it that you each have your own room in the house, and it's a grand affair. You'll see, and I told Cookie to go easy on you. I don't want you overworked like they do you at the hotel. You're Skip's mother, and any lady who can raise so fine a boy deserves a good turn. Don't you think?"

"Please, Mister, don't say no more. You're raising hope when I thought…"

"If you believe in the Lord, Mrs. Johnson, there's always hope. Skip told me you used to read from the Bible right regular to him."

"That was before my husband…"

"I won't take no for an answer, Ma'am. I'll send a man with a wagon over tomorrow. It will be Sunday afternoon. He'll pick you and Skip up, and your things. You can move in tomorrow, and everything will work out just fine."

"The Lord bless you, Mister Temple," said Mrs. Johnson.

"I'll leave you now, Ma'am. You compose yourself, and I'll see you when you get to the ranch."

Skip's mother remained at the table, head bowed, and still crying. The big man silently went out and closed the door.

***

Jim arrived at the dance just as the music started. The schoolhouse was crammed full of people, and there was barely room for the musicians, dancers, and onlookers. People tried sitting in the student chairs and on benches. The desks were laden with drinks, cookies, and pies. Around the dance floor, couples swirled in a tight circle. Big Jim, the tallest man in the room, stood at the back and observed. It was just like he figured. Hazel Workman was the prettiest gal in the room, and there was a line of men arguing and pushing for her attention. He watched her dance five rounds with different young men. In between, others tried to cut in. If Jim hadn't known her, he would not have been able to get close, not even with a club.

On the sixth dance, the rancher made his move. When Hazel saw him, she pushed her way towards him. It was obvious to the crowd and to the men that this tall fellow had taken the lady's favor.

Jim and Hazel touched hands, and the big man guided the schoolmarm out on the floor. Both of them were light on their feet, and they swirled around for several dances. Men tried to cut in, and the strong man blocked them, and so did the lady. Obvious affection showed in their every movement.

Hazel tried to speak to her partner, but the noise was too great. She did manage to shout one response, which he heard.

"It's so good to see you!" she exclaimed loudly.

A song ended, and just before another began, Hazel interjected.

"I need to rest! Let's go outside!"

It was no easy task to push their way through the crowd. Cowboys, ranchers, and young merchants vied for a chance to speak to the pretty schoolmarm—all to no avail. Big Jim had hold of her hand and shoved his way to the door. They walked outside, and the night was dark, cold, and blustery.

"You have to have a wrap," said Jim.

"It's in the house, let me go get it."

Decorum would never allow Jim to enter her home, and he knew it, so he waited. It was only a moment, and she returned, bundled up in a long coat. Her hair had partially come undone, and the wind was blowing it wildly. Jim did not tell her he liked the way it flowed around her head.

"Come on, let's walk away from here," said Hazel, "or we'll never get any peace."

Already young men had come out to seek her company. The rancher took her hand, and they walked away into the night. They followed a path between schoolhouse and home, onto a small street bordered by houses. They continued to walk until they could no longer hear the music. Out of the wind, they slowed and came to a stop.

"I am so glad to see you, Hazel," said Big Jim, looking down at her.

"It didn't seem so. It's been weeks since we first met."

"I'm sorry, I had to move my cattle, hire more men, and work on the ranch. And my hands got rooms ready for Skip and his mother."

"Did she accept the job?"

"I gave her no choice, one of my men will pick them up tomorrow."

"That's wonderful," said Hazel. "I bet she was grateful."

"It took a while. But, once she understood, I think she was pleased."

"If it wasn't for Skip, we would never have met," said the young woman.

"Yes, you're right. And, I was afraid if I came to see you earlier, I never would have gotten my work done."

"Still, it seems to me you took more time..."

"I swear, Hazel, if it had been any other way."

"Sir, your actions don't match your words."

"You know darn well, Hazel, the minute I saw you, you took my breath away. Why I couldn't even speak, I stood there like a big, darn, dumb fool."

"Not in my eyes, Jim."

"Yes?"

"What you did for the boy and his mother proves what kind of man you are."

"I'm glad you think so. If I had the time, I would have come courting, and you wouldn't have had any doubt."

"Is that why you're here now?"

"Yes! You must know how I feel about you. But, it raises a problem."

"What is it?"

"My new ranch is fifteen miles from here. A four-hour ride. There would be no way you could continue to teach school."

"No matter," replied Hazel. "I can't be a school teacher all my life."

Jim, hearing the words, bent down. Forgetting himself, he engulfed Hazel in his arms and kissed her.

"Oh," exclaimed Jim. "I…"

Rather than pull away, Hazel came closer. She closed her eyes and waited for another kiss. He obliged her.

"You do know," said Hazel coyly, "I do insist that you court me in the manner a woman expects. And Jim, didn't you forget to ask me something?"

***

It was the day before Christmas, and Big Jim was in town buying last-minute gifts for his cowhands, and for Skip. He was also going to look for that special ring for Hazel. Running out of cash money, he went to the bank on Main Street. As he approached, three men with bandanas over their faces, revolvers at the ready, came rushing out of the bank. Jim was across the street. The life savings of so many were about to be lost, including his. Jim pulled his pistol and called out.

"Drop your weapons, boys! I got you covered."

A fourth man rode up with three horses. Among prancing steeds, the outlaws tried to mount while firing at Big Jim. The tall man hid behind a narrow post. Several bullets slammed into it, and one grazed the rancher's shoulder. Being a good shot, Jim reluctantly aimed and began firing. He knocked two outlaws out of their saddles, and then a bullet struck the rancher in the chest. The pain was immediate, and he fell. Jim knew this was a fatal wound. As he hit the boardwalk, consciousness began to leave him. His last thoughts were for Hazel, Skip, and his ranch.

***

"The bullet's too close to the heart," said the doctor to Smitty and the schoolmarm. "There's nothing more I can do for him."

Jim heard the doctor but found that he could not move or speak. Strangely, he felt numb but no real pain.

"Oh, doctor!" cried Hazel. "You must save him!"

"It is beyond my skill," replied the physician.

"But who can help him?" asked Smitty.

"If this man lived long enough, perhaps a good surgeon. It would take a steady hand, and it would be maybe one chance in twenty."

"Then send for one!" cried Hazel. "Please, doctor."

"When I examined Jim, I thought he would die with his next breath. It's a miracle that he still breathes."

"It doesn't matter what it costs," said Smitty. "Jim and I got money put away. Why...he got those first two bank robbers, and the merchants stopped the others. You would have lost your money, too, Doc. You owe him. Wire for the surgeon, and tell him any price!"

***

It was a warm place, obscured by fog, which James Temple found himself walking in. Everything was quiet and very peaceful, yet he could not account for where he was. Jim felt like he was drifting, being pulled forward towards a bright circular light in the distance. Yet everything was without pain. He did not quite remember how he had gotten there, or for what reason...then he came to the light.

"Welcome," said a voice.

James saw a bearded figure before him, and he was standing at an iron gate. It was open. Beyond was a stone path, and it looked like it went on endlessly into the distance. The bright light obscured everything else.

"Who are you?" asked Jim.

"I am the keeper of the gate, and I see that you have led a good life—a few exceptions, the war and this latest incident."

"I am beginning to remember," said Jim. "I couldn't help the war, and the robbery was self-defense."

"No need to say more. Let it be recorded that James Temple is allowed entrance."

Then full realization came to Jim, and he remained standing outside the gate.

"Please enter," said the guardian and magically waving a hand, a permanent cross appeared on the back of Jim's hand. "You have been judged, and here is evidence you are placed in heaven."

"No, I cannot. I have to return. Others are counting on me."

"But you must," said the gatekeeper.

"Please tell me how I can go back?"

"Not for five hundred years has any man ever returned to life after coming here."

"Can I make a request?"

"It is most strange that you remember your past life. Being so, since you have not yet entered, I have no choice but to submit your petition."

"Is that all?" asked Big Jim.

"Be warned! You will be judged by both sides. If you lose, your soul is lost. "

"I must return!"

The light dimmed. Everything turned dark, and Jim could see nothing. Then light reappeared. There was a bench with a judge, and to the side was a double row of six seated jurors. Beside Jim at a table, sat Benjamin Franklin. Across from them stood a sinister-looking prosecutor, a representative from Hades.

A court attendant appeared and read loudly from a scroll.

"Hear ye! Hear ye! Now begins the trial for the life of one James Temple. The defendant asks to be returned to the living. His past life will be judged. Should he be found unworthy, his soul will be condemned."

"Your honor?" began the prosecutor. "If I may...I move that the subject be indicted for the taking of lives and be remanded to hell forthwith."

"Objection!" exclaimed Benjamin Franklin. "We haven't heard the circumstances in which these lives were taken. The facts, gentlemen! The facts are what we are after!"

"Objection sustained!" called the judge. "Gentlemen make it short, present your case, and be done with it."

The satanic-looking prosecutor rose and began reciting a long list of deaths. It included Indians, Confederate soldiers, renegades, and the recent bank robbers. Then came a rather impressive summation.

The jury, Jim, and Franklin endured the lengthy argument. And when it ended, the facts seemed to firmly convict the defendant, James Temple.

The renowned defense attorney rose. Benjamin Franklin walked around the table, smiled to the jury, and began listing the good deeds performed by his client. The account was an impressive one with numerous instances of kindness and heroic actions. His summation took an equal amount of time.

Benjamin Franklin concluded with, "Gentlemen, let it be known that James Temple never killed in anger. The fact that he remembers his previous existence is reason enough to return him to life."

"Before I instruct the jury," said the Judge. "Is there anything the defendant would like to say?"

"Your Honor," replied Big Jim. "There are people I love who need me!"

"Jurors," said the Judge. "Do your duty!"

***

Big Jim opened his eyes. It took time for them to adjust. When he did, he saw Hazel and Skip sitting close to the bed, both asleep. Across the room on a bench slept Smitty. Jim remembered the strange dream he had about the light, the gatekeeper, and the trial. It seemed a bit fantastic now, but it was so real. Not wanting to awaken his friends, he closed his eyes and drifted off.

In the morning, when he awoke, Hazel was still beside him.

"Oh, Jim," she said, leaning down and kissing him on the cheek. "You're finally awake. This is the most wonderful Christmas gift a woman could ever have!"

"Are Smitty and Skip still here?" asked Jim.

"Yes, but how did you know?"

"I awoke last night and saw the three of you sleeping."

"You mustn't overdo it," said Hazel. "The doctor said no excitement."

She went out and returned with Skip and Smitty.

"You're awake!" said the boy, coming close to the foot of the bed.

"I am now, son,"

"Are you ever going to be upset!" exclaimed Smitty, grinning. "It cost a fortune to hire that surgeon. And on Christmas Day! You've got one big whopping bill!"

The injured man struggled to sit up. He began to laugh, then grabbed at his chest and winced in pain.

"It was worth it, don't you think?" he said.

"It sure was," agreed Hazel and Smitty in unison.

"Was the bank money saved?" asked Big Jim.

"Yes," replied Smitty. "The merchants came out after you shot, and finished off the other two fellers. The money they took went right back in the safe."

"Good," said Jim. "Then I can pay the bill."

"Now that you mention it," said Smitty, "I have a withdrawal note. You sign it, and I'll run it over to the bank. That doctor wants his money before he leaves."

"How much did he charge?" asked Big Jim.

"The doctor said not to upset you," exclaimed Hazel in alarm.

"How much?"

"A thousand dollars!" shouted Smitty. "You got to understand it was him or death. And it was Christmas

Day."

"Three years of cowboy wages?" said Jim, moving and then crying out in pain.

"The banker said you could afford..."

"Let it go, Jim," said Hazel, "he did save your life."

There was a long silence, and then Jim motioned for Smitty and the paper. The rancher signed and watched his friend wave to Skip. Together they left the room. Big Jim looked down and saw the cross on his hand. Instantly he realized that what he thought was a dream was very real. Then the injured man smiled.

"Hazel."

"Yes, Jim?"

"After we're married, I have a story to tell you. One you may have trouble believing."

Hazel came up close to the bed, reached down and kissed her man gently on the lips. Then she took hold of his hand.

"Why not tell me now, Big Jim?"

"No, I think I'll wait for the right moment. But for now, how about another kiss?"

TO LIVE OR TO DIE
Kit Carson vs. Porcupine Bear

Knowing that a momentous occasion of conflict was about to transpire between warriors, the Devil appeared on the Great Plains of the American West. An observing angel saw Satan materialize and walk upon the earth. Something fateful and imminent was transpiring. The Angel quickly discerned what was occurring and descended.

"Ahh, it's you." exclaimed the Devil.

"You expected no interference? You underestimate the Lord's persistence. I have come to ensure you do not tip the scales in your favor."

"Go to Hades!" blurted out the dark entity.

An aura of light increased around the Angel, and then it spoke, "Not likely."

To the living souls below, both the Devil's and Angel's presence went unnoticed.

***

Dark surrounded the open prairie as deep and thick as black ink. Clouds in the night sky blocked moon and stars.

The wind blew, and in it, the promise of moisture and a growing storm. In the darkness, a tiny fire glowed, giving warmth and comfort to its maker. The small flames could be seen miles and miles away.

A Cheyenne Dog Soldier saw the fire and knew that some white man was beside those flames, daring nature, daring all that lay hidden in the darkness to come and attack. Either the man was new to this country and unaware or was some tough frontiersman looking for a fight. On a journey to purify his spirit, Porcupine Bear would not ignore this challenge. He would seek guidance from the Supreme Being to help him overturn his expulsion and banning from the Dog Soldier society.

The warrior had killed one of his own, Little Creek, in a fight. He must find atonement. He cursed the whites for the fire-water that made him crazy and caused his friend's death. Porcupine Bear, the shamed Dog Soldier, was seeking strong medicine. Nothing would keep him from returning to the warrior society and leading them. The whites and their growing invasion must be stopped. Perhaps this intruder with the fire was his first step back to his tribe.

Not familiar with the country and not having come this far south before, the Cheyenne knew it was dangerous to travel in the dark. One misstep and he could fall into a deep arroyo or over some steep cliff. Even if his horse could gallop through the darkness, they would never reach the fire before the storm came. Shrugging his shoulders, Porcupine Bear guided his mount up a hill and slid to the ground. There were fallen trees everywhere. He led his pony to the shelter of a lone cottonwood. He secured his paint with hobbles, and for extra measure, tied it to the tree. Then he went looking for cover. He found a fallen log with an opening under it. Placing large pieces of bark from the dead tree, he improved his shelter. It may not block all the rain but most of it. By daylight, the storm would pass, and he would ask his maker to help him find and kill that white man.

From far away came rumbling, it gradually increased and moved closer. Lightning began to cross the distant sky. The wind blew with terrific force, and with it came sporadic drops of rain. Then the storm swept in upon the Indian and his mount. Terrific bolts of lightning struck all around, and thunder clapped, deafening man and beast. With the white flashes, the land and sky turned to daylight and back to intense darkness. Rain fell in a flooding torrent. Despite his shelter, Porcupine Bear became drenched, and he heard his horse scream. Breaking its horsehair rope, the paint, despite its hobbles, hopped away.

"Maxemaheo, do not forsake me! Great Spirit, save me from this storm, let me fulfill my prophecy. Let me lead my people once again against the invaders!"

The storm lasted until morning, fiercer in intensity than anything Porcupine Bear had ever encountered. Towards the end, lightning struck the lone cottonwood where the horse was once tied. The force blasted the tree in half. The sound made the Indian's ears ring in pain. The burning tree briefly lit up the darkness around him before rain put the flames out. The smell of burning wood and ozone struck his nostrils, and it was not pleasant.

Slowly the lightning and thunder lessened and moved off into the distance. The rain continued for some time, decreased, and stopped. Then came an eerie silence. Chilled to the bone, the warrior wanted to get up, gather wood, and start a fire. But he knew it was hopeless, everything was too wet. He would spend an uncomfortable morning with a moist elk skin wrapped around him. Perhaps by mid-morning, he would be able to make a small fire and go look for his horse. He knew he would have to walk through thick mud to find him. A warrior in this country, without a mount, was powerless.

"Why, Great Spirit, have you allowed this to happen?" asked Porcupine Bear. "Must this punishment continue?"

***

The plainsman, Kit Carson, stood before his fire when he heard the storm coming. He hobbled his horse secure in a copse of trees. Then he laid out his bedroll before the warm fire and staked down the canvas cover. His rifle and possibles bag were secured beneath it. A tent might blow away, but by slipping down under the waterproof tarpaulin and onto his blanket, no matter how hard it rained or how hard the wind blew, he would remain dry. The frontiersman knew the fire was a luxury only a greenhorn would start. But this night, he was chilled, and he didn't care if man or beast came to take him.

The storm moved relentlessly forward upon Carson and his horse. It was the worst he ever experienced, and the sound of thunder and rain under the waterproof cover was deafening. Once in a while, Kit Carson raised a corner of the canvas and was amazed at the unending flashes of lightning illuminating the dark land. To keep from suffocating, he lifted the cover for fresh air. Heavy rain splashed inside, forcing him to stay put. It was a long time before the storm passed, and the frontiersman worried about his horse. But he remained where he was, knowing full well that with this much rain on the hard adobe, that it would turn to sticky clay. It would take a few days for it to dry out.

Carson understood that any man or animal that saw his fire would be hard-pressed to reach him now. It was a foolish thing for him to announce his camp. But he was aggrieved at life. He came on this trip deliberately to defy man or devil. It was unbearable to be around civilization after what happened. Watching his Arapaho wife, Singing Grass, give birth and die, was more than any man could take. Until he got his balance back, he dared fate to confront him. Here on the plains of Colorado, he would find himself, and heaven or hell be damned.

***

The Devil delighted in the massive thunderstorm he started and the discomfort it caused the two humans. It was the Spirit above that dissipated the storm. The two men below represented the never-ending conflict between right and wrong. Both omniscient parties watched and tried to remain neutral.

"Their souls will soon be mine," exclaimed the Devil.

"That is yet to be seen," replied the Angel.

***

It took two days for the hot sun to dry out the wet adobe ground. Porcupine Bear and Kit Carson forced themselves to remain at their camps and wait. The Dog Soldier found his hobbled horse at the bottom of the hill, covered in mud. He removed the restraints, and both man and beast had a hard time reaching the camp. Great clots of wet adobe collected on their legs as they climbed. The warrior had to stop and scrape mud before continuing on.

Both men, in their separate camps, lit small fires and cooked and ate rabbits they managed to snare. Carson was able to brew coffee, and Porcupine Bear drank water. Through the remaining hours, each chewed on tough meat and contemplated their futures. That night they slept on the ground and suffered troubled dreams. The faces of the many men they killed, and those friends who died, remained in their thoughts. Intermittently, they awoke, wondering what their destinies would bring. Both prayed to the creator to end their inner conflicts and put them on the right path.

***

The two plains fighters left their camps at the break of the third day. Each was motivated to travel across the land, eager to meet his own fate. Porcupine Bear rode south toward where he had last seen the fire, the night of the storm. Kit Carson took a northerly direction following the Huerfano River and skirting Greenhorn Mountain. Near both horsemen, the giant Spanish Peaks rose three miles into the sky.

It was noon when they spotted each other from a distance. They crossed the open plain, riding over parched yellow grass, and avoiding large clumps of jumping cholla. The two headed directly at each other. Both determined they would meet and deal with what their maker brought them.

Kit Carson was a man with a keen mind who never forgot a landscape or the ground he had ridden over. His ability to track and guide others in the great West had given him early fame. Porcupine Bear, a former leader of the Dog Soldiers, never forgot a face and seldom ever, a name. The rider coming towards him was a diminutive man, and he looked familiar. Seeing his reddish hair, and eventually his blue eyes, the Indian recognized a worthy adversary, Kit Carson.

Not more than thirty feet away, both riders halted their horses.

"Haaahe!" said Carson in fluent Cheyenne.

"Hello, white man, Carson," said Porcupine Bear, in broken English.

"You know me? You speak English? Ne'-tonesevehe (What is your name?)"

"I am called Porcupine Bear."

"I have heard of you."

"And I, you. Once I see you, little man. My people say you small but fierce fighter."

"And I was told you are a big man among Cheyenne Dog Soldiers."

"You know such things?"

"I talk Cheyenne, Spanish, and five other Indian languages. Some tribes are my friends and some not."

"Big smart man."

"I don't know about that, but I hear you are a great warrior."

Porcupine Bear winced. This white man did not know of his troubles with his band, and he would be the last to tell him.

"You are far south from your people," said Carson. "What brings you here?"

"I seek."

"Looking for someone?"

"Hova' ahane! (No!)

"Then why a Dog Soldier here, alone?"

"On medicine journey."

"What medicine?"

"We fight, little man."

"If so, give me a reason."

"You whites come. Take buffalo, land, kill our people, never keep word. We stop you."

"Reason enough. But why me?"

"I kill Carson, become his strength. Big medicine for me, for the people."

"I'd rather not fight you. Suppose we each go our own way?"

"You small, ugly, yellow dog. I cut you into pieces."

"You won't find it so easy," said Carson.

Porcupine Bear reached for his weapon. Carson threw himself from the saddle and onto the ground, pulling his Colt-Paterson. The Cheyenne warrior threw a tomahawk with blinding speed, knocking the pistol from Carson's hand and numbing it. Then he put heels to his pony and rode forward, jumping onto the little man before he could draw his second revolver. The men rolled and fought upon the ground. Carson was small but fast and wiry. He twisted from the Indian's grasp and instantly came to his feet, a knife in his hands.

"Sneaky man-fighter," said Carson's opponent.

"Not so bad yourself," replied the famous frontiersman.

Porcupine Bear pulled his trade knife from a beaded sheathe and grimaced. The two men circled, and the Indian stood inches above the diminutive foe. The Cheyenne thrust and Carson parried. Metal on metal clanged. Then each man tried to make a slicing cut, leaning, thrusting, and twisting back and forth out of reach. Finally, the Dog Soldier made a swiping slice and cut open Carson's buckskin shirt, and blood flowed. Ignoring the pain, the wounded man dove forward and underneath the Indian's thrust. The blade went deep into Porcupine Bear's right shoulder, and he dropped his knife. The Indian's wound bled profusely. Holding his shoulder, Porcupine Bear tried to stop the bleeding with his left hand, but it had little effect. Losing blood, the Dog Soldier became dizzy, went to his knees, and then lay flat on the ground.

"You fight well, Carson," said Porcupine Bear. "Finish it."

"No," responded the frontiersman, and then he grinned, exposing fine yellow teeth. "No need. We both win. You're cut, and so am I."

Kit Carson, bleeding extensively, went to his horse and

opened a bag. He took out bandages he always carried, along with needle and thread. The frontiersman approached the prone Indian and went to his knees.

"Don't touch, white man!" ordered Porcupine Bear.

"Don't be a fool! We both need to sew up our wounds, or we'll bleed to death."

"No!"

"It was a good fight. We both proved our mettle. Lie still."

Kit Carson picked up his knife and began cutting away at the Indian's vest. Porcupine Bear grabbed the man's buckskin shirt, but his grasp was weak, and he passed out from loss of blood. Carson worked quickly, and taking a prepared needle and thread began sewing the shoulder wound shut. He had trouble with the flowing and slippery blood but managed several stitches. With difficulty, feeling weak, Carson continued to work on his adversary. He placed cloth pads against the wound and wrapped a tight bandage around the Indian's upper chest and shoulder. This was not the first time the plainsman treated such a wound. The warrior's bleeding lessened and stopped.

Stripping off his own shirt, the frontiersman, with great effort, began sewing the deep cut in his chest. With only one bandage left, he formed a pad across his wound, found a leather string, and tied it tight. Then he too lay flat on the ground and rested.

Hours later, towards evening, Kit Carson awoke. He saw that the Cheyenne warrior was still unconscious.

"Now what do I do?" he asked out loud.

Feeling weak, he managed to stand. He walked to

the horses and stripped them of their Indian and Western saddles. Finding hobbles, he struggled to attach them. Then he grabbed his canteen and drank. As he moved about, Carson had to rest frequently. Over time, he managed to lay out the Indian's elk hide and gently shove the bigger man onto it. Unrolling his own bedroll, the plainsman laid down. He chewed on jerky, and despite his thirst, left the remainder of water for his wounded adversary.

Porcupine Bear's face turned dark red, his skin beaded with sweat, and he began to mumble. A fever was rising, and it wasn't long, and the Indian was completely out of his head. He began moving around, the wound opened under the bandage, and blood flowed. At first, Carson tried to hold the bigger fellow down but had no success. Unable to stop the bleeding, the frontiersman started a fire. He heated the Indian's knife, removed the bandage, and applied the red tip to the wound. Flesh sizzled, smoke rose—but the bleeding stopped. Smiling grimly, Carson put the knife down, picked up his canteen, and poured water over the other man's face. He tried to get the Cheyenne to drink but to no avail.

This went on all night, and Kit Carson finally decided to tie up his enemy in an effort to keep him from moving. Exhausted, the frontiersman crawled back to his bedroll and slept.

In the morning, the hot sun shone down upon Carson's face, and the heat awakened him. Thirsty, he dare not drink the last of the water. Instead, he went to his foe and examined him. Porcupine Bear was still burning with fever. Pouring a few drops of water on the warrior's face, the frontiersman tried to get him to drink.

For the remainder of the day, the plainsman rested and did his best to care for his wounded enemy. The next morning, it looked doubtful that the Dog Soldier would survive. He was feverish, weak, and constantly mumbling strange things in Cheyenne. For certain, they would both die if they didn't have water. Struggling with the saddle, Carson gave up. He removed the hobbles, grabbed reins of his horse, and mounted. Holding the Indian's empty leather water skin and his canteen, he rode for the Huerfano River. He returned and administered to Porcupine Bear as best he could.

"Lord," said Carson out loud, on the fifth day. "If you see fit, save this man's life. I've done all I could."

At dawn, Carson awoke, and looking to his enemy, he saw him lying there, eyes open, and his fever gone. The plainsman picked up a canteen and slid it over to the thirsty man. Building a fire, he boiled jerky and mashed it into a type of broth. When it cooled, the hungry Indian drank it down. After a time, Porcupine Bear struggled to sit up.

With several attempts, the Dog Soldier finally whispered, "Why?"

"I guess," said Carson, "to live and fight another day."

"No, tell me why?"

"At this moment, isn't it enough that you live?"

That evening, Kit Carson took his rifle, went hunting, and came back with a mule deer. With the fresh meat, the two men slowly recovered. During that time, they hardly spoke to each other.

A few days later, the two plains fighters put together

their packs and gathered their horses.

***

"You had no right to interfere, they both should have died," protested the Devil to the hovering entity.

"It was a fair fight," said the Angel. "Both men were looking for redemption."

"If you would not have been here, their souls would have been mine."

"Not true. With such brave men as these, their destiny is their own."

"This is not over. There will be another time."

The air clapped loudly, and the Devil disappeared. Looking down, the Angel smiled and slowly ascended.

***

Kit Carson and Porcupine Bear saddled their horses. Both men mounted and started to ride away, and then the Dog Soldier turned his paint to face his enemy.

"Again I ask, why did you save me, white man?"

There was a long silence.

"I don't rightly know. Something told me we had a good fight, and if I could, to save you."

"Was it the Great Spirit?"

"It could have been," replied Kit Carson.

"It is a shame to owe you my life, Carson. But if it was the Great One who told you, then that is a good sign."

"Yes, a good sign for both of us," said Carson, studying the stern face of his enemy, and then he smiled.

Porcupine Bear, in formal manner nodded his head.

Carson did the same, and they turned their horses and rode in different directions.

Dear Reader,
If you enjoyed reading *The Soul Gatherers: Thirteen Western Tales,* please help promote it by composing and posting a review on Amazon.com.

Charlie Steel may be contacted at cowboytales@juno.com or by writing to him at the following address:

Charlie Steel
c/o Condor Publishing, Inc.
PO Box 39
Lincoln, Michigan 48742

Warm greetings from Condor Publishing, Inc.
Gail Heath, publisher

CPSIA information can be obtained
at www.ICGtesting.com
Printed in the USA
BVHW031615010621
608544BV00001B/41